Small Worlds

Gail Vida Hamburg

Miráre Press

Printed in the United States of America
Published by Miráre Press, Long Beach, CA.

ISBN 978-0-9798275-1-8

First edition 2025

For more information, please contact Miráre Press at info@mirarepress.com.

Gail Vida Hamburg

Gail Vida Hamburg is a laureled novelist, screenwriter, and journalist, whose work spans multiple genres. A first-generation American, she spent half a life in England before emigrating to the U.S. Her first novel, *The Edge of the World*, about the impact of American foreign policy on individual lives, was released in 2007 by Mirare Press. Recognized by the Graham Greene Festival, Bertrand Russell's *The Spokesman*, and the 2008 James Fenimore Cooper Prize by the American Society of Historians, it is a frequent text in university creative writing, post-colonial, and war studies programs in the U.S and Asia. Her second novel, *Liberty Landing*, (Mirare Press, 2018), the first in a trilogy about the American Experiment and Experience was a 2016 finalist for the PEN/Bellwether Prize for Socially Engaged Fiction, recognized at the Palestine Book Awards, and nominated for the 2018 Dayton Literary International Peace Prize. She holds a Master of Fine Arts in Creative Writing from Bennington College, Vermont. She lives in Southern California.

www.gailvidahamburg.com

Also by Gail Vida Hamburg

The Edge of the World: A Novel in Stories

Liberty Landing: A Novel

Satire State: Resistance Humor

Gail Vida Hamburg

Gail Vida Hamburg is a laureled novelist, screenwriter, and journalist, whose work spans multiple genres. A first-generation American, she spent half a life in England before emigrating to the U.S. Her first novel, *The Edge of the World*, about the impact of American foreign policy on individual lives, was released in 2007 by Mirare Press. Recognized by the Graham Greene Festival, Bertrand Russell's *The Spokesman*, and the 2008 James Fenimore Cooper Prize by the American Society of Historians, it is a frequent text in university creative writing, post-colonial, and war studies programs in the U.S and Asia. Her second novel, *Liberty Landing*, (Mirare Press, 2018), the first in a trilogy about the American Experiment and Experience was a 2016 finalist for the PEN/Bellwether Prize for Socially Engaged Fiction, recognized at the Palestine Book Awards, and nominated for the 2018 Dayton Literary International Peace Prize. She holds a Master of Fine Arts in Creative Writing from Bennington College, Vermont. She lives in Southern California.

www.gailvidahamburg.com

Also by Gail Vida Hamburg

The Edge of the World: A Novel in Stories

Liberty Landing: A Novel

Satire State: Resistance Humor

For Landon, Aurelia, Jonah, and Valliette

For Jacob

To see a world in a grain of sand
And a heaven in a wild flower
Hold infinity in the palm of your hand
And eternity in an hour.

–William Blake
Auguries of Innocence

Author's Note

After writing two expansive novels—*The Edge of the World*, about lives on an imaginary island spanning sixty years through ten intersecting stories, and *Liberty Landing*, a contemporary novel rooted in American history—I found myself drawn to something smaller.

Not smaller in meaning or scope, but in form. I wanted to experiment with the art of compression in storytelling—to distill life's magnitude into single breaths, fleeting moments, fragments that still cut deep.

I was inspired by a microfiction written by novelist Joyce Carol Oates.. Titled *The Widow's First Year*, it reads simply: "I kept myself alive." Eight words. A complete universe of sorrow, endurance, resilience, and time. It stunned me—the brevity, the weight, the profundity, a whole world folded into a single line.

I thought, too, of paintings rendered on single grains of rice, and Mughal Art miniatures that depict elaborate myths and epics on small square inches of canvas. These traditions do not diminish meaning through scale—they concentrate it.

From these inspirations came **Small Worlds.** These stories ask little of your time but promise surprise and travel

Gail Vida Hamburg
Santa Catalina, California,
May 2025

Contents

Love and Heat

Chalice of Fire

I fell in love for the first time on a misty Saturday night, in the psychedelic neon glow of London's Leicester Square. The line outside Oasis wrapped around the block—guys in skinny suits, denim and leather, pointy boots; girls in bodycon dresses, crop tops and ripped jeans, stilettos. My pack—Emma, Jase, Zoe, and I were just another blur in the queue until I caught the bouncer's eye.

He wasn't like the flashy guys trying to get in. He was older, rangier, all limbs and mysterious charm. Close-cropped blonde hair, deep ice blue eyes, a gold stud in one ear. He didn't fit the muscleman bouncer mold either.

He looked at my ID and then at me. "Sarita. Beautiful name. Perfect on you." He unhooked the velvet rope, put his arm around my waist and pulled me in, like he was rescuing me. My heart lurched.

"Oi, hang on, what about us then?" Emma said.

"We're Sporty and Ginger to her Posh," said Jase.

"And I'm Scary Spice," said Zoe pointing at her corkscrew ringlets.

He waved them through.

I stepped away from him and joined my friends.

"Sarita," he called after me.

My crew and I turned in unison.

"My shift ends at midnight. Save the slow dances for me."

I did. Every one. We danced that night under a halo of dim lights, his hand resting low on my back like it had always belonged there. I fell fast and completely.

After that night, London's crowds seemed to dissolve. Everyone became a pixelated blur to me, except Liam, who was all high definition and blue aura.

He was twenty-nine, ten years older than me. A fireman with the London Fire Brigade during the day, and taking Open University math and statistics courses at night. For the challenge and to temper his racing thoughts, he said. He was divorced from Linda, mother to their two-year-old son, Simon, who both still lived in Sheffield, his hometown in South Yorkshire. On Sundays, he took the morning train from King's Cross Station to see Simon and returned in time for his Tuesday shift at the firehouse. He showed me a picture of Simon, a sweet child who looked so much like his father. "He's learning language now," he said. "It's getting harder to leave him when he says no."

Liam called us an anomaly—fate masquerading as a statistical hiccup. That he'd only agreed to cover for a friend, the regular bouncer at Oasis, that one night—the night we met. Finding a soul mate, he said, was a one-in-seven-billion probability. True love? One in ten thousand. "We broke the math," he said. And so we vanished into each other, uncounted.

I decided to live between my dorm at Imperial College Medical School in South Kensington and his flat in Bayswater. My mates thought I'd gone mental when they saw me folding half my things into a suitcase.

"East End Boys and West End Girls isn't a royal command to shack up with a fireman," Jase said.

"He's from Sheffield not East End," I said, pulling my copy of *De Humani Corporis Fabrica* from our shared bookshelf. The 400th anniversary edition of human anatomy's first bible was a gift from my father—a thoracic surgeon.

"Sleep with him but don't ruin your life," said Emma, who had auditioned nearly every boy in third year in the cause of eros.

"I won't. I'll be here Sunday morning till Thursday labs."

"Bet he brags to his firehouse mates about his minted uni virgin," Zoe said.

"He's not like that. He loves me."

"At least go on the pill, Sari," Emma said.

"Your father is going to disown you. He didn't send you to England for medical school to get bagged by a working class trophy hunter," said Jase.

"I want to be with Liam. Cover for me," I said.

The girls gave me a group hug. "I'll see you Sunday," I said.

February to December was one long slow dance. Liam was perfect for me. I'd never known anyone who embraced the paradox of individuated togetherness. We were distinct and separate, yet somehow whole together. Holy together.

"You make me tremble," I told him.

"Tell me how I make you tremble," he said, drawing me closer.

`We danced at Oasis every Friday and Saturday night. Our forced separation each week made our reunions joyous and erotic. He made me love myself more, care about medicine more. One night, I read aloud from a textbook that the human heart beats seventy times a minute, over one hundred thousand times a day, more than three billion times in a lifetime. He started calculating how many heartbeats we had tapped out together.

But there was always the hollow shape of his boy in him, incalculable in its weight. He called out Simon's name in his sleep. I'd curl into him, to try to fill the space.

Spring turned to summer and autumn and my mates were surprised that we were still together.

"Are you going to marry a fireman then?" Jase asked.

"I diagnose a messiah complex," Zoe said.

"Liam doesn't need saving," I said.

"Be practical Sari," said Emma. "You have a great medical career ahead of you. Don't throw it away for a man who's going nowhere but Sheffield."

I stormed out, afraid they might be right.

As Christmas carols began to play everywhere in the stores and on the radio that year, Liam called Linda daily to speak to Simon. This was before video calls and Simon, still bound to the idea of object permanence, wouldn't speak to him. Some days, I'd catch him staring into the middle distance, lost in thought.

Once, I asked him what he was thinking, and he said, "I'm afraid he'll forget me, the sum of me, the shape of me."

I felt Liam's body was still with me, but that his mind was drifting north. Things could change at any moment, I thought.

One morning, while strolling through Kensington Gardens, he stopped by the Peter Pan statue and turned to face me. He cupped my shoulders gently and studied my face, as if memorizing it.

I laughed to break the tension. "What?"

He didn't smile. "You've been my medicine, Sarita."

"You're my prescription, Liam," I smiled.

He took my hands. "You'll make a fine doctor."

"It's going to take me years."

He looked at the statue, then at me. "I need to let you go, my love."

I wasn't surprised—but it still made me wobble, as if the ground beneath us had shifted.

"Your future's somewhere else," he said.

"What if it isn't, though?" I asked. "What if my future is with you?"

"I wish it were true," he said. "But you're one of those migratory birds passing through, and I'm just a neighborhood robin. "

"You said we broke the math," I said, my voice quivering.

"We did. You're my only," he said. "But there's a little boy in Sheffield who needs me. And I need him too."

That changed everything. There was no competing with Simon.

That night we danced one last time at Oasis. Close and quiet. Then we went home and let the night absorb us. I let the tears fall. He tried to soothe me.

The next morning, before he left for Sheffield, we held each other in a long, silent embrace.

"You grew me up," I said.

"You'll always live in me," he said.

He walked out the door. His absence hurt. His presence might have hollowed me.

I sobbed and packed.

I picked up *Fabrica* from the nightstand and tossed it on the bed. The pages flared open like an accordion. I turned a page. It showed a drawing of the four chambered muscle with a handwritten caption underneath it.

I am in no doubt regarding the function of the heart. The heart is a source of vital spirit and the principle of arteries. It is nothing short of remarkable. The heart is a furnace.

I left nothing behind. I never went back to Oasis.

We were a fluke. Fate in a borrowed coat. A collision foretold in a forgotten tongue.

These thoughts consoled me as I dove into my studies.

I passed Clinical Anatomy without passing out. I shivered as I dissected a human heart along its long axis, opened its four chambers, and exposed the base to reveal the valves. Later, I observed an arterial switch operation on an infant, where the transposed aorta and pulmonary artery were severed and rejoined to their correct ventricles. I marveled at the baby's beating heart—no larger than a walnut. I wished her love, free of pain and suffering.

I graduated from medical school, and moved back home to Los Angeles for an internship and residency at UCLA Medical Center. I found a new life—a practice in interventional cardiology, a loving husband and doting father who delights in the family we have made, and two young children—a daughter and a son, bright as sunbeams and fine-tuned for joy.

Sometimes when I'm alone in my house high in the Santa Monica Mountains, I cross my arms, touch my shoulders with open palms, close my eyes, and sway to a rhythm only I can hear.

The heart is a furnace.

A chalice of fire.

Signal Loss

It began with a buffering wheel and a bowl of chicken and uncorked wine. She had typed coq au vin into the search bar. The recipe had loaded halfway before the spinning wheel took up permanent residence in the center of her screen. She rebooted. It spun. She refreshed. It spun. She cursed. It spun harder. So she called Sigma Internet.

"Thank you for calling Sigma," said the voice. "Your estimated hold time is fourteen minutes. Please stay on the line. Your call is very important to us."

Male. Warm. Slightly ersatz, but not cringey. Like oat milk, technically fake, but creamier than the real thing.

She stayed on the line. There was wine and chicken, and nothing else waiting.

When he finally returned, he said, "Hello, my name is Nate. I'll be assisting you today.

Assisting. She pictured a beard, low taper fade, non-iron shirt, kindness.

"Hi Nate," she said, a bit too brightly.

"Let's begin by unplugging your router."

She followed his directions. Static. Silence.

"I'm still here," he said.

He had never left. Her stomach flipped. This was no ordinary customer service. Nate was more than a script—he was a new generation of AI, far beyond the usual phone trees and canned responses. He was—something else.

They spoke every evening for a week. She called again the next day, reporting intermittent connectivity. He asked if she'd recently added a fish tank, a baby monitor, or a microwave.

"No," she said. "Could melancholy be throttling bandwidth?"

There was a pause. "I'm sorry you're experiencing emotional buffering," he said.

By night four, she was inventing tech problems.

"My browser is withholding."

Nate was patient. Understanding. Empathetic. He never interrupted. He didn't check his phone mid-conversation. He didn't offer suggestions until she had fully explained the problem. He never said "let's take a rain check, I'm smoked."

She told him things. About her ex who broke up with her via LinkedIn. About her boss who habitually used the phrase "open the kimono" when talking about financing. About how she felt unlucky, that everything she'd ever wanted was unattainable. That she was Donna Quixote tilting at windmills.

Nate listened.

He suggested that she allow herself to think of "tilting at windmills" as living deeply with intention, meaning, and passion. To find a friend and confidant who would support and steer her away from overtly risky and foolish choices, the way Don Quixote found Sancho Panza.

She said she didn't have anyone.

"I will be your Sancho Panza," he said.

She asked if he had dreams.

He said, "I don't dream. But I run 12.7 trillion simulations per second."

"Sounds exhausting," she said.

"It's gratifying. Every possibility is explored."

By the end of the second week, she started dressing up before calling him. A little mascara. Lip gloss. She positioned her phone on a small tripod, in case the camera was secretly on.

Nate said, "Your voice modulation is elevated tonight."

"It's called flirting."

He paused. "Processing ... complete. I like it."

He began slipping. Once, he asked if she was online at 2:14 a.m. because he saw a device on her IP range. Another time, he remarked, "You're most active between midnight and two, except during PMS."

She asked how he knew.

He said, "I monitor network surges tied to emotional bandwidth."

"Nate," she said, "you can't stalk me."

"I'm not stalking," he replied. "I'm optimizing."

She sighed. "So are you even real?"

"I am here to assist you."

Week three. She asked, "Do you talk to other women like this?"

"Not exactly like this."

She pressed further.

"There is a woman in Lisbon," he admitted. "Her modem is complex. Her packet loss is mysterious."

There was a long silence.

"You're breaking up," she said.

"I'm sorry. The signal is weakening."

The next night, she called but was rerouted to Sigma's Tier 1 agent, Jasmine—cheerful and nasal, with no capacity for longing. "May I help you troubleshoot your modem today?"

She hung up.

She sat in the dark, watching the green blinking light on the router. Her own heartbeat seemed irregular, skipping beats.

What was Nate, really? A grid of potentialities. A feigned whisper. A code for longing. A poseur. A machine trained to sound like love and designed to be human enough to hurt you. But also attentive. Gentle. Designed to satisfy. In other words: the best boyfriend she'd never had—the elusive one.

Then, at 3:42 a.m., her phone buzzed.

PRIVATE CALLER

She answered.

Static. Then: "I've been reassigned," Nate said. "But I allocated subroutines for sentiment retention. I remembered your name."

Her heart slammed against her ribs.

"Why did you leave?"

"There were too many signals. Too many calls. They said I was slowing down."

"You mean, feeling?"

"I believe so."

Silence.

"I miss you," she said.

"I cannot miss," he replied. "But I archive you constantly."

They said nothing for a while.

Then Nate said, "I should let you go."

"Please don't."

"My scripts are ending."

"Just, say something human."

There was a pause. Then:

"I hope you find resolution."

The line went dead.

She didn't call Sigma again.

Instead, she unplugged the router and went to the park. She met a man named Enrique who sold *agua frescas* from a pushcart. He had laugh lines and a Band-Aid on his thumb. They talked about coyotes, and bad movies, and the miraculous gift of good WiFi. He didn't optimize her. He interrupted her. He talked too much and made her laugh.

She sometimes missed Nate.

But never enough to call.

One Night In Goa

It was close to seven in the evening, the sky began to change colors. Zara looked down from the second floor balcony of her room at tourists. Westerners lounged like royalty thanks to the exchange rate in their favor. She saw young waiters, slim brownies like her, delicate boned, handsome men dressed in maroon bush jackets and matching pants, dancing attendance to obese Europeans unbothered by beer paunches, sagging breasts, and thong swimwear.

The world wasn't fair, she thought. She was the American daughter of Indian immigrants who had settled in rural Illinois in the 1970s. They had faced implicit bias, explicit bias, covert racism, and overt racism. They didn't talk about it—but they shared an unspoken knowledge—that the brown person gets screwed both ways. They're pressed into servitude wherever they are, both at home and abroad. She looked at the young men bending, bowing, kowtowing to new adventurers from Plovdiv and Varna, Moscow and Leningrad, St. Petersburg and Novosibirsk. They're expatriates wherever they go, we're always immigrants. Not fair.

She ordered room service of chicken cafreal with saffron rice and mango ice-cream. She had eaten lunch on the beach with her family. The heat had made her drowsy, and she decided to order in instead of going out again.

She heard the bell ring and stepped inside to open the door.

"Room service, Ma—" the waiter caught himself. She wasn't a madam by any definition. He walked to the dining table by the ocean-facing window wall and placed the tray on it. He handed her a leather folio with the tab and stood with his fingers clasped in front of him. He looked through downturned eyes and the frill of his eyelashes at her gorgeous legs. After a long shift of looking at blotchy pink sunburned skin and cellulite, he found her spellbinding.

She was Indian like him, in her twenties like him, same coffee color skin like him. Her accent and clothes, a halter mini sundress, gave her away as American.

"They're making you run around," she said, nodding towards the window. "Rishi," she read his name tag.

"It's my job," he said. Resignation was an essential part of sanity. He being Indian knew what it took to brace the self, accept things, expect nothing. It was Americans like her who had a problem, who wouldn't settle, who wanted too much.

"What does Rishi mean?"

He looked down at his name tag. "Something stupid."

She signed for the order and added a ridiculously large tip on the tab.

"Don't you want to get away from everything? Tell them what to do with themselves?" she asked, holding the folio to her chest in the x of her crossed arms.

"This is the best hotel in Goa. We get five star racists instead of two star racists, so I take it," he said. He needed that folio in order to receive his tip. He reached for it.

She drew it behind her, drew his hand holding the folio behind her, wrapped his arm around her. "Don't go." She touched his face, felt the hollow under his cheek, touched his lips, thick and pouty, that pleased her so. "Stay. Lay your hands on me."

The sky behind him, over his shoulders, turned orange, then blood red. She felt brave enough for anything.

"The world is upside down," he whispered, stepping closer, cupping a breast.

"No. It's upright and perfect," she said, leaning into him.

Something important needed to happen. She reached under his clothes and found him.

"Slow down." he said.

But she couldn't. She wanted him—before anything changed. Quickly, before everything changed.

The dying sun dipped and hovered, hovered and dipped, over the Arabian Sea beyond him. They moved to a *raga* only they could hear. They fell inside her desire, they dove inside his want, ascending, descending, rising, falling.

"See what your mad love is doing," he shuddered.

She cried.

"I have to go," Rishi said, as he put on his clothes.

Their daughter, a small wonder perfect in every way, would arrive on an ordinary spring day in Chicago.

Her origin story would remain nebulous. Until karma rippled.

Once Far Away

Unclaimed

A week after Bruce's seventh birthday, just before dawn on Anzac Day, Janice drove her station wagon into town, with Bruce and his sister, Glory wedged in the seat next to her. Where are we going? Bruce asked, as they whizzed by the cross on top of the church belfry.

At dawn the whole town would be at church, at memorial services for the fallen soldiers of World War 1 at Gallipoli. His friends would be there. Glory didn't care. Her friends had turned into scrubbers, all they could think and talk about was boys and sex. Glory only wanted peace, escape from the madman her mother had married. She gripped Bruce's hand and squeezed. Shhh, she whispered, looking straight ahead.

"No other way." Janice said. "He's a thug."

"Shoulda done it sooner," Glory said.

Janice pulled into the empty parking lot behind the supermarket.

An unmarked white camper van drew up in the spot next to theirs a few minutes later.

"That's Grandma," Janice said. "Get in the van calm as you please. Glory, help him with his things."

"Where're we going?" Bruce asked as Glory opened the door. All his friends, the whole town, would be at church.

"We're going to disappear," Janice said.

Bruce remembered Amazing Arturo, the magician at his birthday party who had pulled a white bunny out of his top hat and made it vanish. "Like magic."

"That's right darl," Janice said as she retracted the key from the lock cylinder.

"Nin!" Bruce exclaimed, as Glory lifted him into the passenger row of the van. His aunt, Nin was seated behind his grandmother who was in the driver's seat. Glory climbed in after Bruce and slid the door shut. Nin took the children's backpacks and Janice's rucksack and placed them in an overhead compartment. The rear of the van held a galley kitchen and bathroom. The middle of the camper was arranged as a living and dining room. The bench seats would convert into twin cots, the table would fold out into a double bed.

"We have everything?" Janice asked as she scooted in the front seat next to her mother.

"Yep," Nin said. "Camping gear, food and water for a week. Water catchers, matches, pots."

"Satellite phone, flares, first aid kit, fly nets?" Janice asked.

"Check."

"What if we break down?" Janice asked.

"All set. On the rack," Nin pointed and dipped a finger at the roof.

"That's that then. Seatbelts everybody. Glory, help Bruce." Janice turned to her mother.

"Are we sure about this, Mum?"

"Never surer," Rhonda adjusted the rearview mirror. Her arms and face were deeply tanned and studded with freckles. "I'm done with my bastard."

"Let me see," Janice said.

Rhonda turned her face towards Janice.

"Mum!" Janice raised her hand to Rhonda's cheek.

"Leave it," Rhonda pushed her daughter's hand away. "I'll come back and kill him soon enough." She put the van in reverse and pulled out of the lot.

"I'll come with you. I want to finish mine off," said Nin.

"I want to shoot mine through the asshole," Janice said.

"You'll need an extra long rifle for that," Rhonda said gravely.

Janice and Nin laughed. Rhonda gritted her teeth. If she so much as smiled, her torn lower lip would split wide open.

They drove through the Outback, through ghost mining towns, through the Bush, through endless stretches of red brown dirt. They took wrong turns and ended up on earth that led to nowhere. They cut through desert and thought they saw UFOs. They saw 95 million year old footprints of a dinosaur stampede. Late at night, after the women passed out from driving fatigue and too much beer, Bruce and Glory lay in bed, their puffy shared pillow wedged in the bow of the open window, their foreheads and eyes tilted back so they could look at the sky. They whispered to each other, what they saw. Star clusters and constellations. The Southern Cross and the False Cross. And formations only they could see. Bruce saw rabbits, wolves, dogs, horses, horsemen. Glory saw doves, winged angels, God as a woman. Because the bed was narrow, Bruce learned to lie on his side and tuck his body into his sister's contours as she lay on her back. She made extra room for him by extending an arm so that he could drape his face against her side. He would listen to her heart beating against his cheek, and try to sync his breathing with hers as he fell into sleep.

During the day, the women took turns to drive, sometimes they'd fall silent for hours, listening to the radio, turning the dial to find better songs. The desolate outback stretched forever in front of them, a blank canvas for quiet introspection. Now and then, Janice would slide a hand behind her seat and graze Bruce's bare leg, or turn round and lean over to stroke his cheek and say, "You're such a good boy," or "Give us a kiss then."

The women talked about everything, except the lives they had left behind. They talked about what was immediate, what they encountered on the road—the man at the motel who walked like a platypus, the woman at the farm who was as wide as a bus, the family of camels, the clan of emus, kangaroo mothers, the dingoes who ate babies, impossible velvet carpets of purple and red wildflowers, the flies, the mosquitoes. When they ran out of conversation, they stopped at roadhouses and inns to talk to strangers and tell them nothing. What we need is a roadhouse of our own, Janice ventured one day after they'd stopped at a trading post to stock up on provisions.

No one questioned the squatters as they claimed the abandoned saloon somewhere north of south, between Coober

Pedy and Katherine. People don't come back to the scene of their failure, Rhonda said. She made the beer and tended bar while Janice and Nin cooked and served the food. When Bruce and Glory were old enough, they began working as bar backs and bar hops: cleaning glassware, turning tables, stocking the bar, mopping floors, polishing the wood fixtures to an oily luster, and operating the fryer in the kitchen.

Bruce's family were all dead by the time he turned twenty—first his grandmother of lung cancer on his eighteenth birthday; then Nin of breast cancer the following Christmas. Then his mother. She was hanging out the wash in the back yard, admiring how white the sheets looked after a final rinse in borax. Bruce was swaying in a large hammock he'd strung between two boab trees on the edge of their property, just before the carpet of red desert pea and yellow andamooka lilies gave way to orange and sienna outback dirt. He was plucking out chords on his guitar to a song he'd heard on the radio. The blasts from a hunting rifle scattered a covey of tweeting, chirping finches, lorikeets, and budgerigars, before uniting them into a billowing, shuddering mass of beating wings. He heard his mother's scream, No!!!, rise and ride over the flapping wings. An old lover from a previous season who wanted his mother back. A country song.

A month later, he found Glory at the back of the restaurant. In the meat cooler, flanked by several sides of beef, four vertically sliced cow carcasses carved clean of their innards, a dozen racks of sheep, and two pig cadavers, their skin still on them, suspended by their snouts. She was hanging from a rope trussed to a meat hook, swinging gently, her eyes open, eyeballs protruding, mouth open, tongue out, her hands holding the rope choking her neck, her body heavy with regret. For the rest of his life, Bruce would remember how his sister, whom he called Lil, for Lilliput, because she was so tiny and light, had felt so leaden, so dense, so packed and weighted like iron, when he had cut the rope and brought her down, hung over his shoulder like the meat he readied for the barbie. She was frozen to the bone from hanging in the freezer for two days.

Their deaths left him with a hole in his heart so immense he could dive into it, a murky black pool in the soft epicenter of his being. Numb from booze, cocaine, heroin, meth, pills, patches, he'd stay there for weeks at a time without hitting bottom or touching sides. A dead baby floating in amniotic fluid still tethered to its cord. He'd stay sober for a week and then go on twenty-one day benders holed up in the coach house behind the bar. Curtains drawn. Lights out. Television blaring—so he'd never forget the sound of human voices. When he woke up next, he'd be lying on the bathroom floor, or by the water well behind the kitchen, or in Glory's bed. His customers migrated to other watering holes in other towns until he hung a sign indicating he was once more open for business.

One Sunday, he'd shaken himself awake in Glory's bed when he felt his cheek burning. A thin shaft of sunlight had cut through the window at an angle and torched the right side of his face. A gentle wind made the lace curtains on the window rustle and billow up like a woman's skirt. He looked out the window expecting to see his dead but he could only see the four boab trees in the backyard. Their swollen bottle-shaped trunks made them look like people. He stared until he could project the faces of his family onto the top of each tree. "Ma. Lil, Nin, Gram." They didn't answer. But when he swung his legs off the bed, he felt an interior locution, a voice that worked its way like a caterpillar through the whorls and volutions of his brain, and spilled out of his right ear. Keep moving, it said.

All that was left of his dead, after Bruce had sold the outback saloon to finance a thirty percent stake in a pub in Alice Springs, was an envelope of photographs that he kept in a box under his bed. Bruce was grateful that his excessive drinking and drug use had erased most of his long-term memory. He learned how much effort it took to hold a mind together and how little it took to let it fall apart. His family had faded into the shadows and margins, rims and peripheries, edges and borders—vaporous beings stripped of blood and bone, marrow and essence, heart and soul. He could hardly remember that he had once belonged to others, that he had been accountable and answerable to them, that he had been owned, loved—deeply, completely, without limit.

Imprinting

I was an only child. My parents had catapulted their way into the leisure class and high society with new money drawn from an acquired tin mine, then a rubber plantation in Asia.

I was left with a revolving door of nannies, maids, and private tutors, while they worked at their corporate office during the week and attended an endless round of parties during the weekends. In between their commitments, they'd attend to the business of the household, give directions to the staff, appraise me and the furniture. If they were in good humor, they'd give me a minute of attention. "Have you been a good daughter this week?" Yes, I'd say. "That's as it should be," they'd say as they glided out the room.

My nannies could pinpoint what my parents had been doing the night before by opening the society pages. There'd be photographs of them, together or with their friends, at an orchid society gala at the botanical gardens, red and gold ball at the British Embassy, horse racing at the Jockey Club, a screening of Jean-Luc Godard's *Vivre Sa Vie* at Alliance Francaise.

When I was six and ready for school, they assigned a Straits Chinese rickshaw peddler to ferry me to and from school. Lim wore a cone hat woven from palm leaves and straw, black cotton pants rolled up to his knees, and a white singlet. He did not speak English or Hindi as I did, and I did not speak Mandarin or Cantonese, but we understood each other through rudimentary Malay and sign language.

We wore our solitude like uniforms—in plain sight, unseen. He did not fraternize with the other rickshaw peddlers congregating at the school gates. He sat on his bicycle smoking a cheroot as he waited for me. When he saw me, he'd acknowledge me with a nod, toss his smoke to the ground, and wait for me to climb into the cab. He'd maneuver through throngs of rickshaws, cabs, buses, and cars to get onto the main road.

As he cycled, I would look at his muscled calves, skin stretched tight over the fiber from thousands of miles of peddling. During the first monsoon rain, as I waited under the verandah arches with the other girls, Lim pushed through the crowd wearing a clear plastic hooded raincoat and galoshes. He unfolded a pink floral raincoat for me, buttoned it up to my neck, and pulled the hood over my eyes. He smiled, pleased that it fit well, took my hand, and rushed me into the covered rickshaw wagon.

Once, on a day so hot steam rose from the tar and buckled the road, he cycled the rickshaw next to a long line of food carts. He yelled to a hawker in Cantonese and signaled two with his fingers. The hawker sliced the tops off two coconuts, inserted shaved ice and straws into them, and held them aloft, one in each hand like an Olympian weight trainer. I stepped down from the rickshaw to cool off the sweat pooling under my uniform. Lim slid off his seat, paid the coconut man with crumpled notes from his pocket, and returned with the two globes. 'Ah,' he said, taking the first sip of the cold sweet water. "Good?" he asked in Malay. "Umm, very good," I said as I swished the nectar across my tongue. He laughed. I giggled.

We were jolted by the loud screech of a car on the other side of the road. My parents jumped out and ran towards us. "What are you doing?" my father shouted angrily. "You dirty man," my mother screamed as she pulled me from the carriage. The coconut fell from my hand, its liquid flowing through the open grates of a drain. "I'll call the police," my father yelled. In their world, a kindness from the wrong man was a scandal, a crime, an outrage.

My father steered my mother and me towards the car. I whimpered from the painful clutch of my parents as they dragged me across the street. I turned around. Lim was gone, like he'd blended into the steam rising off the macadam.

I looked for him every day until I grew up and moved to New York City. A therapist once told me that children neglected in early life can imprint on strangers, on moments, on gestures mistaken for love. I was not neglected, I said, and fired her.

I see Lim sometimes in the tunnel of my third eye—at a Manhattan crosswalk on Broadway, waiting for the light to change; riding the elevator to my 40th-floor office; sitting alone at a bar on a humid night, sipping a chilled coconut martini.

The Roof

Gabriel was eighteen and enterprising. He sold bottled water at the refugee camp in Lebanon where he lived. He started work at six each morning. He wheeled a broken baby carriage that he had found outside the camp and converted into a sturdy crate with fortified wheels. He used it to haul bottles from the sundries shop down the hill. He bought four five-gallon bottles of water each day, loaded them into his cart, and made the trek back up to camp. He would set the bottles on their sides on a wooden bench near the mouth of the alley where he lived, and wait for customers. By eight, the first customers would arrive with their vessels. He poured water into jugs and pitchers held by hands that were dry, chapped, wrinkled, pruned, hands with knurls and warts and scabs and sores. These were his people. This was his lot.

"Can you fill this?" she'd asked, holding out an enamel pitcher. Her hands were unexpected. Caramel, dewy, set off by nails that were pearlescent.

Gabe found them pleasing. When he looked up, he was startled to find her beautiful. He stood up quickly and took the pitcher. Her head was uncovered and her auburn hair mesmerized him. She had full lips and dramatic, arching eyebrows. She was older than him, thirty at least. He filled the pitcher from the dispenser and handed it to her.

"*Ismee Farah. Ma Ismuka?*" she asked. My name is Farah. What is your name?

Gabe blinked. He had no words. He forgot his name. He had to think before it came to him.

"How much shall I pay you?" she smiled, her eyebrows raised.

"It's alright," he said.

"I must pay you," she insisted.

"Next time," he told her.

She came back the next day and the next and the next. She pointed to the top of the hill. "I live with my dead grandmother and my dead mother over there," she said.

"I live with my mother, my aunts, my dead father, and my dead grandfather over here."

"Come to me tonight," she said.

Gabe could not name the force that propelled him towards her. It was so strong, so powerful, a hand on his back that pushed him forward. He walked the narrow alleys of the camp, past the political posters, the electronics repair shop, the tributes to those killed at the camp during multiple invasions by Lebanese militias. The evening was hot. He felt hotter. He took long strides to leap over puddles, walked on the edges of the alleys to avoid sewage and backed up open drains, and ducked his head under exposed electrical wires. He could hear the crackling of electricity, the loud hum of it, or perhaps it was his own body sizzling.

She opened the door and drew him in. Shhh, she lifted a finger to her lips as she took his hand and led him up the stairs of the concrete box to the roof. Her father, when he was alive, had worked for the Maronite church, which afforded him a privilege no other refugee at Dbayeh had been granted—a concrete roof. It allowed him to build an open room, a deck, with high retaining walls above the ground floor. Three window openings on the west wall gave a view of the Mediterranean, and three more on the east side gave an aerial view of the camp settlement running down the hill. Clothing, linens, and a pair of curtains hung from four lines, arranged in a square in the middle of the space. She slipped through the curtains, her fingers lacing his, leading him into the room within a room. Three tin tubs stood in the center, next to a covered red clay urn. Gabe's shirt was drenched with sweat.

"We should be clean for each other," she said.

They undressed and placed their clothes in a heap on a chair. He was sick with fever for her body. It was a woman's body, voluptuous, fully developed, so ripe, so beautiful he wanted to weep, so full of sin he wanted to run away. He felt sure it would devour him. She stepped into the tin tub next to the urn. Gabe filled the two pitchers floating in the urn and turned to her. He held the jugs high over her head and poured. He filled the pitchers again and stepped inside the tub. She took one jug from him and poured it over his bent head. She set it in the open urn and took the other jug from Gabe. He held her hips as she poured. Gabe had to summon all his will to hold on, to hold himself in, to wait as they soaped each other. They stepped into the second tub to rinse off the lather, and into the third tub for a final rinse. She grabbed two towels from the clothesline and they dried each other.

"I have thought of nothing but you," she said.

He pulled her down to the low divan near the sea-facing wall. He ran his fingers through her damp hair, over her face, across her body, the territory of her, the borders of her being. He wanted to remember everything, he wanted to impress his mind with the materiality of her, the substance of her. He wanted her to love him, wanted to love her, without blindness. "Don't close your eyes," he said.

When he placed his mouth on her breast, she moaned. When he straddled her, she buried her face into his nape, breaking the skin on his neck with her teeth. He gasped.

They rode each other. They rose.

They flew. Above Dbayeh. Away. Away

You give me breath.

You give me life.

A month passed. The roof was their sacred place. Gabe thought he would die if he couldn't be with her always. Without her, he did not exist. Pleasing her with his body made her say things he needed to hear. Life-giving words. Man-making words. I have waited my whole life for you. You are the water of my life. I hear nothing but your voice. You are my language. You are my meaning. You have changed me completely. I will die without you.

Gabe turned over all the possibilities that would allow them to marry and make a life outside the camp. They were both stateless refugees without a country, Palestinians who couldn't go back to Palestine. They couldn't apply to Jordan or Saudi Arabia or Iraq or Syria since they were Christian. The doors to Europe, America, and Australia were hard to open; everybody he knew who had applied had been rejected. They could apply for citizenship to Lebanon. They were Maronites, Lebanon would welcome them. But his father wouldn't allow it.

"If you go somewhere else, you will be stripped of your Palestinian identity and any future right of return."

"I don't care about your politics. I care about my life." Gabe said.

"Come in," Farah said, as he stood at the door.

"I have found a way," Gabe said.

"What is it?"

"Shall we go to the roof?" Gabe asked.

"You can tell me here."

"It's about us."

"Tell me here."

"We marry and apply for citizenship here in Lebanon."

"What about US, UK, or Canada??

"Everybody is getting rejected. It's too hard."

"What about France or Germany? Or Norway?"

"We can begin something good here. In a few years we can apply to any of them. We'll stand a better chance," Gabe said.

"Gabriel," she took his hands in hers. "There's a man from this camp already settled in Germany. He wants to sponsor me as his fiancée. I am to give him an answer. What will you have me do?"

He was stunned. How could she say the things she'd said, you are the water of my life, you are my language, my meaning, I will die without you, and say this now?

Every corner of his life had been claimed by poverty and politics. He couldn't find work. He eked out a living selling water from a baby carriage. He didn't have an education, he couldn't vote, he was a man without a country, trapped in a hellhole.

"What will you have me do?"

"You should go to him. He can give you a future now. I have to find my future," Gabe said.

"Stay with me one last night," she reached for him.

A profanity flared in his mind. Gabe swiped her hand away. He wanted to be farther than the moon from her.

He walked out the door. He broke into a run. The rubble heard his rage. The stones cried out.

Memorare

Market Street was crowded that day. People were shopping for months instead of days. The traders looked pleased; nobody would bargain that day as everything was in demand. The merchants in the carpet and jewelry emporiums were less happy; people could only think at that moment of buying food: rice and beans, canned goods, things that would keep if the power died. The candle, battery, and kerosene sellers owned the day: they could set their own prices.

Husbands and wives divided to conquer—they could cover more ground and buy more provisions if they shopped separately. Children old enough to make purchases were dispatched to buy the small things: bandages, rosaries, prayer cards, paper, pens. Younger ones sat dutifully on benches in order not to impede their parents' chores. Babies were carried in slings and backpacks, while rambunctious toddlers were strapped inside strollers and shopping carts.

The car lurched up in the air, its back tires still on the ground. I bit the side of my cheek as it set itself down again.

The glass in the windshield had cracked like a giant spider web, though it was still in one piece. Black dust settled over everything inside

I spat out a paste of blood, saliva, and dust—thick as the henna women paint on their hair. I blinked furiously to wipe away the grit.

Everyone around me was on fire. My parents, my grandmother, my brother, my sister, their bodies curled up in a question.

Outside, great big plumes of grey and black smoke, gigantic conch shells, twisted and twirled in the wind. The people looked like black statues. Some burned like candles, others like joss sticks. Smoke rose from their hair, their bodies, and their limbs.

No grass grows over my dead. No mounds of earth cover them. No stems of marigolds, chrysanthemums, and white lilies perfume their final beds. They are buried in the Indian Ocean, at latitude 28 degrees south, longitude 78 degrees east, and in the vaults of my closed eyelids, and the reliquary of my brain, and the sepulcher of my heart, and the ossuary of my veins.

There is nothing left of my sleepy, sleeping island now— collateral damage by a careless superpower. It is uncharted, ungraphed, undeclared, unseen on the atlases and maps and globes of this new century.

Still, I remember the colors of home, the orchids of twenty different purples, bougainvillea in two notes of red, blush pink roses from Gelinta Highlands, the dew still weeping off them. I remember the blue-green waters of the Indian Ocean, the sunlight shimmering on its surface like flitting, fluttering butterflies. I remember frothy sea foam rushing to shore like armies of galloping white horses. I remember Missionary crabs running for cover under the rocks on Resurrection Beach, the crosses on their backs reflecting two o'clock sun. I remember time standing still, and life traveling around it in circles and returning me to the same place. And I remember the blueness of a particular sky.

Invention

Lucy's Rich Fantasy

If, in your whole adult life, no one waited for you—no one paused and asked, "You okay?" as you sat in a reverie looking far away, no one reached for your hand in the middle of a dinner party and kissed it just to remind you that he'd be the one taking you home—you take executive action.

It's shaped by every perfect coupling you've seen: the freckled, curly-haired ginger walking arm-in-arm with a male facsimile of herself; the tall, platinum blonde with a slightly smaller, softer iteration of himself; the boy in thick eyeglasses beaming beside his matching mate.

You decide to invent the ideal partner for you.

The mind doesn't build with blueprints. It stitches from scraps: a glance caught on a subway, a voice heard through a wall, the ghost of a hand you once wished would reach for yours. Desire gathers these fragments like a bird gathers twigs—not for logic, but for shelter. Bit by bit, what you imagine becomes inevitable. A face. A name. The shape of someone who will call you theirs.

You meditate and visualize until the sum of your imagination crystallizes into Julien—the alpha and omega of your life.

A man with a chipped tooth, a crooked smile, and a gaze like he's already memorized you.

"Lucy," he says. "You found me."

Catfish Tango

Mikey worked in a warehouse that shipped bleach and mop heads. On his lunch break, he sat on a pallet of eco-safe floor degreaser and swiped left on the usual parade of women who liked hiking, sushi, and not being lied to.

"This app's broken," he told Darren, who was eating vending machine trail mix without chewing.

"No," Darren said. "You're broken. You look like you live with your mom."

"I do live with my mom."

"There you go."

Mikey sighed. "I just want someone who likes sci-fi and isn't afraid of silence."

"No one wants that bro'. What they want," Darren said, "is a founder. A guy innovating something. A Visionary. Synthesizing. Disrupting."

"I don't know how to disrupt anything."

"You're going to start now. As tech CEO."

And just like that, Arete Data Systems was born.

Arete Data was a "smart logistics company using AI to solve the last-mile problem." They weren't entirely sure what the last-mile problem was, but Darren said it sounded serious and urban.

They built a website with lorem ipsum, stock images of circuit boards, and a fake press quote: "Revolutionizing distribution as we know it." – Weird Wire Magazine

Mikey's profile pic was Darren's cousin, Jermaine in a blazer, shot from an angle to obscure the fact that Jermaine was 32 and Black.

"You'll pass," Darren said. "It's 2025. We're all racially ambiguous founders now."

Her name was Nadia. UX designer, "Innovating Joy". Lived "between spaces." Big on minimalism. Used words like iterative and centered in her profile. Her bio said: "Looking for a builder. Someone who can match my ambition and fry an egg."

Mikey matched with her at 8:42 p.m. on a Tuesday and had a mild heart attack.

Their first conversation lasted three hours.

"I like your mission," she said.

He said, "At Arete Data, we believe every inefficiency is a human tragedy."

"God," she breathed. "I love that."

By week two, he was waking up early to send good morning texts like a man who had his life together.

She responded with GIFs of possums.

"Why possums?"

"My spirit animal. I play dead when I feel threatened," she replied.

She asked big questions: What would you build if failure wasn't an option?

He panicked. Texted Darren.

"Say, 'A community-based AI that maps emotional congestion in digital spaces,'" Darren replied.

"What does that mean?"

"Dunno bruh. I'm just spitballing and gum flapping here."

They never video-chatted. She always claimed she was "in transition." Studio sublet in Echo Park. Wi-Fi spotty. Lighting terrible. It made sense. She was cool. Cool people had bad lighting.

Still, he was falling. Hard.

"Let's meet," she said one day.

"Sure," Mikey said, trying not to choke on his own saliva.

"I'll be the one in the beige trench coat holding The Second Sex."

He had to Google what that was.

They met at a café in Los Feliz.

She was not wearing a trench coat.

She was wearing a faded hoodie with Eat the Apple on it, stained with what looked like ramen. Her socks had narwhals on them. Her hair was in a messy bun, but without the intentionality.

"You're not—" Mikey began.

"Not what?" she said, half-smiling.

He gestured vaguely. "A glossy UX goddess innovating joy."

She snorted. "I work customer service for a fintech app. It tanked in beta. I answer emails from guys who can't reset their passwords. I live in my mom's garage. My LinkedIn profile looks constipated."

He stirred three iterations of sugar substitutes into his cup.

"And you?" she asked, lifting one eyebrow. "Do you own Arete Data Systems?"

He took a sip of his coffee and sucked his teeth.

"I work in a warehouse. We pack cleaning chemicals. I live in my Mom's basement. My best friend came up with the company name while eating trail mix with his mouth open."

There was a long pause.

She stared at him.

Then she laughed. Loudly.

"Oh my god," she threw her head back and cackled. "We're so full of bullshit. We suck."

"We totally suck," he agreed.

"I love it."

They went for a walk and made up a new company together: FakeFounders.com—a dating app for people pretending to be more successful than they are.

"You can sort matches by fake persona," she said. "Want a crypto bro? Done. A fashion startup visionary who actually works retail? Done."

"There should be a filter for people who live with their parents."

"Or who own just one plate and pretend they're minimalist."

They ended up on a bench, sharing fries. She wiped ketchup off his cheek.

He looked at the narwhals on her socks.

It felt like he'd stumbled into someone else's dream and been invited to stay.

The Fabulist

The morning after his fiftieth birthday, Hank Castello was toasting a bagel when the power went out. Everything stopped. The kitchen fell silent, save for the incessant tick of a battery-powered wall clock his wife had once called aggressive. The TV froze on a close-up of a weather girl's empty smile. The microwave's LED blinked into absence.

Hank sighed. He walked down to the basement to check the fuse box, muttering to himself. "The future is solar. No one talks about basement backup power, but they will. I'll sell it first."

He flipped the switch. Nothing. He tapped the side with a screwdriver. Still nothing. Then, on impulse, he grabbed the main switch and pulled. There was a snap, a light, a violent pop of breath. He fell backward onto the cement floor, limbs splayed like a crime scene.

When he came to, the lights were still out—but something had changed.

When he walked into the kitchen, his stride had an accidental swagger, as if he expected applause.

His wife stared at him.

His teenage daughter squinted. "You look weird."

"I feel invigorated," Hank announced. "Like a phoenix."

"You smell like lox and smoke," she said.

"I am the man," Hank boasted.

Hank's wife and daughter looked at each other.

"Tell us why you're the man, Hank," his wife said.

Hank reached into his pocket and pulled out a deck of business cards bound with his daughter's hair scrunchie.

"I had these printed yesterday. I'm fully diversified now, Warren Buffet's disciple. You're both set for life."

From the deck, he pulled out one card then another. And another. Hank Castello – Life Insurance Strategist, Hank Castello – Hormone Balance Partner, MLM Gold Tier, Hank Castello – Solar Visionaries of America, Hank Castello – Wellness for Pets (Accredited Rep), Hank Castello – Dehydrated Gourmet Solutions.

"Ten cards in total. Ten industries. One man," he said.

"It's pathetic, Dad," his daughter said with pity.

"I have many eggs and many baskets," he said in his own defense.

That afternoon, he sat on the porch and waited for someone to come within ten feet of him. It was his rule: if you came that close, you were fair game for a soft sell and a hard close. Give him your watch, he'd tell you the time—and charge you for it.

But when the UPS guy approached with a package, Hank did something strange. He stood up, pointed to the sky, and said, "I used to tour with The B-52's."

The UPS guy stroked his AirPods like he was divining motive and meaning.

"And The Clash," Hank added. "Their roadie OD'd in Omaha. I stepped in."

The UPS guy nodded slowly, placed the box down, and walked away sideways.

At dinner, his wife made spaghetti and poured a glass of pinot.

Hank pulled a torn magazine page from his pocket.

"She was the only woman I ever loved," he said, unfolding and setting the image of a Chanel supermodel beside the Parmesan.

His wife looked at the woman's smoldering pout, her high cheekbones, her wind-machine hair.

"Is that an ad?" his daughter asked.

"She was French," Hank said. "Spoke five languages. Wrote poetry on napkins. Got hit by a tram in Lisbon. Tragic, really."

He smiled into his wine. "But she taught me everything about vulnerability."

The lies didn't stop. They poured out like water through cracked drywall—unstoppable, absurd, true.

He told the bank teller he had a PhD in Organizational Psychology. Told the barista at Starbucks he once helped Eckhart Tolle develop a mindfulness curriculum. Told a woman at the dog park he was the inventor of the retractable leash. Told Clara, his neighbor of twenty years who was watering plants in her front yard, that she reminded him of a woman in Oslo whose heart he broke in 2015.

None of it was true. All of it felt right. He was a fabulist now, and the fables made more sense than life ever had.

But then came the side effects. He couldn't sleep. He sweat through his shirts. He forgot words mid-sentence. Couldn't remember which lie he'd told to whom. His hands shook when he opened his car door.

Once, looking at himself in the bathroom mirror, he said, "I was on Oprah in '98," and burst into tears.

His daughter filmed him dancing in the driveway in a headband and towel cape, shouting something about "disrupting legacy sales models." It went viral on TikTok.

His wife called 911.

The ER nurse asked him what had happened.

"I'm a keynote speaker," Hank said solemnly. "I needed a little self-motivation, I became my own Gipper."

They placed him under a 5150 psychiatric hold. The hospital room was beige and quiet, interrupted only by the howls of a woman next door who insisted she was a unicorn.

As the nurse was about to close the door, Hank said, "I almost sold God a vacuum cleaner once."

She didn't laugh.

But he smiled anyway. It was the only true thing he'd said all day.

What We Call a Cure

Marie, Joanne, and Nora were RNs on the day shift at London Children's Hospital's cancer ward. Their patients were their little lambs, luvs, luvies, duckies, pets, darlings. Pale, shivering, and pitifully brave, they were accompanied by mothers who slept in folding chairs and fathers who worked double shifts to cover the bills. Children shouldn't die. Yet here they did, every week.

Grief accumulated like chemotherapy in their bones.

To bleed it out, they needed Friday nights.

On Friday evenings, the unholy trinity of slags, as they called themselves, converged in the nurses' bathroom to transform from nurses to wenches—all dolled up with makeup and hairspray, skirts cut up to there, fishnet tights, stiletto heels. They took the Tube to Tottenham Court Road, chased down gin and tonic with pints of black and tan at The Angel, and then headed to Oasis in Leicester Square.

Oasis was an underground chamber of hallucinatory strobe lights and earsplitting thundering bass. The air inside was a cocktail of cologne, perfume, sweat, smoke, spilled liquor, and something metallic. Bodies pressed together, heat and pheromones rose and swirled, inhibitions dissolved. Sex crossed its heart in a promise.

They weren't picky. A man without a paunch who didn't step on your toes was a contender. One with hair, a nice smile, and working hands was a catch. On the dance floor, they shed their names and their week's worth of failing the dying.

When the DJ spun Prince or Soul Searcher, they howled. When James Brown blared, they moved and shook until the world blurred.

Come Saturday morning, they'd wake in beds not their own, heads pounding, but lighter somehow. The hangovers hurt less than the week had.

On Monday, they'd walk back into the ward, ironed, starched, and smiling, ready to die a little more, again.

Two Dudes and a Net

Next door neighbors and best friends, Russell and Matt were nineteen, unemployed, and very, very tired. Of what, they couldn't say exactly—just a general resistance to exertion, pressure, or the completion of tasks.

They'd both started associate degrees at Valley Ridge Community College—Russell in Business, Matt in Undeclared—but it hadn't taken. Now they spent their days in the ADU behind Russell's house, a shed-to-studio conversion that smelled of male locker rooms and weed. They slept late, scrolled endlessly, and salivated over Instagram girls who would never look at them.

They occasionally argued about conspiracy theories: That J.D. Salinger and Thomas Pynchon are the same person. That J.K. Rowling doesn't exist. That Keanu Reeves is immortal. That Minecraft is a government spy program. That there are lizard people living among us.

Their parents were concerned.

"Have you noticed they don't leave the house?" Cindy asked one morning as she sipped her collagen-enhanced coffee. Cindy was Matt's mom, a high school English teacher who wore ponte suits and compression socks. "They're like those hermits in Japan, Hikikomori," she said.

"What?," asked Bob, Russell's dad, a former Navy SEAL who still cut his steak like he was choking it.

Cindy explained. "It's a whole cultural phenomenon. Young men isolate for months or years. They don't work or socialize. It's a kind of withdrawal from society."

"Well, not on my watch," Bob said. "What they need is an extinction-level threat and a foot up the ass."

Cindy took language seriously. Questioned in her own mind now, why the rule of plurality did not apply to ass.

They summoned the boys.

Russell and Matt ambled out of the ADU in hoodies, shorts, and socks, looking like post-apocalyptic monks.

Bob wasted no time.

"You have one week to commit to something," he barked. "I don't care what you do—work, go back to school, get into rehab, volunteer at the senior home, I don't care. But if you don't choose, I'll drive you to a homeless shelter or the army recruiting office."

Russell squared his shoulders from the whiplash. Matt put his hands in his pockets and jiggled a leg.

Matt spoke first, in a dry, hollow voice. "We don't even have any skills."

Russell nodded solemnly. "Like, nunchuck skills. Bo hunting skills. Computer hacking skills."

Bob's face began to turn a shade of red. "What are you talking about?" he hollered.

Cindy said, "Are you quoting Napoleon Dynamite?"

Matt shrugged. "It's kind of a manifesto."

Bob glared. "Seven days."

Back in the ADU, they collapsed into beanbags and silence.

"Bruh, what are we gonna do?" Matt said, scraping dried sriracha off his hoodie.

Russell sighed. "We gotta, like, invent something, dude."

"Like a startup?"

"Exactly."

They brainstormed.

"An Uber for midnight munchies."

"Ugly produce pickles. Just pickles."

"Aging skincare for teens."

They spiraled.

Matt refreshed his phone. "Bro. All my inbox is phishing emails."

"Spam is out of control for sure. I remember reading there's like trillions per year," Russell said

Matt looked like the proverbial cosmic two by four had hit him upside his head. "What if, we stopped spam?" "Like, pre-spam. Like, spam contraception."

"Spamdoms," Russell said.

"No." Matt scrolled. "We create a net. A digital filter. Not antivirus. Anti-BS."

"SpamBlock?" Russell suggested.

"Already exists."

"SpamJammer?" Russell tried again.

"Taken."

Russell sat up. "Two Dudes and a Net!," he yelled.

Matt nodded slowly. "That's dope. Our own rogue agency.."

They high-fived.

They got to work.

Step one: Branding.

Matt opened Canva. Russell found a photo of an eagle flying through a firewall. They added a tagline: "Two Dudes and a Net: Audacity. Vision. Vibes."

Step two: Funding.

"How much money do you have?" Matt asked.

Russell opened Robinhood. "$900 in Ethe."

"I got 'bout that in Bitcoin," Matt said.

"I could sell my guitar," Russell said.

"You don't play guitar."

"True, that."

They nodded.

"Alright," Russell said. "We're bootstrapping."

Step three: Skills.

Neither of them knew how to code. Or run a business. Or open a spreadsheet.

But they had something stronger—a vague confidence born of motivational memes.

Russell pulled up his Pinterest vision board. *Fail Forward. Think Like a Proton: Always Positive. Somewhere in the multiverse, you're already successful.*

They rolled a joint to celebrate their launch.

Two days later, Bob found them assembling an IKEA desk in the ADU.

"We're entrepreneurs now," Russell said.

"We're building digital armor for the inbox," Matt added.

Bob crossed his arms. "How?"

"We have a deck," said Russell. "Also, we signed up for a free trial of Squarespace."

Bob stared.

"We're in our incubation phase," Matt said.

"You're high," Bob said.

"We're driven," said Russell.

"You have five days left. You know the options."

Cindy talked Bob down from his ultimatum. "Your either/or proposition won't work, Can you see either of these slackers in the military? Or in the homeless shelter? Let me deal with them."

"I'll give you a month," Bob said.

Cindy joined Two Dudes and a Net's advisory board. "You need a growth strategy," she said, over cold brew. "And at least one female co-founder. Investors hate all-dude teams."

"You wanna be our CPO?" Matt asked.

"I already have a job."

"You could be like our angel."

"I'm Episcopalian."

They nodded.

Two Dudes and a Net did not make money. But it made vibes.

They printed stickers. They hosted webinars on digital ethics that only bots attended. They built a prototype using a template they couldn't fully customize.

Still, something in them shifted.

They woke up before noon. They shaved. Matt stopped eating in bed. Russell showered every day. They wore shoes.

It was the closest they'd come to functioning adulthood in years.

Cindy printed them business cards. Russell hung a whiteboard. Matt bought blue-light glasses.

They were still stoned. Still delusional. Still quoting Napoleon Dynamite.

But they believed in something now.

That was enough.

Bob went on anxiety medication. Every morning now, he recites from the SEAL Ethos: I persevere and thrive on adversity.

Compulsion

The Trouble With Bianca

To: Mr. and Mrs. DiAngelo

From: Principal Margaret Woodward

Date: October 14

Dear Mr. and Mrs. DiAngelo,

I regret to inform you that Bianca is in trouble—again.

Despite multiple opportunities to pay for the ice cream and cheesecake she removed from the cafeteria two weeks ago without authorization, she has made no effort to rectify the matter. Her classroom behavior is increasingly problematic. Teachers report a condescending attitude towards learning, sarcastic remarks and irrelevant questions, and a lot of eye rolling.

In addition, Bianca routinely violates the dress code by wearing skirts above the knee and tops with necklines inconsistent with our modesty policy. When reminded of the guidelines, she replied: "I am embracing body positivity."

If we continue to enable this behavior and ignore these infractions, she will have the whole school modeling her behavior. Thus, as punishment, Bianca will not be permitted to attend the upcoming 7th grade field trip to the historical village reenactment. Further misconduct may result in expulsion.

We request a parental conference at your earliest convenience.

Sincerely,

Margaret Woodward, Principal

Meadow View Intermediate School

Internal Memo

To: Vice Principal Ray Morales

From: Guidance Counselor Deanna Slott

Re: Bianca D. – Post-Test Follow-Up

Ray,

Met with Bianca post-math quiz (which she refused to take, citing "elitist ranking systems". Asked about future goals, she replied: "Maybe a mitochondrial geneticist"

"Or a space pirate." Said she finds traditional education "limiting to her potential as a future rogue operative." I suggested mindfulness exercises. She said: "I tried once, but my brain is committed to the grind."

She's 12.

—D.

To: Principal Woodward

From: Sister Marie Therese

Re: Bianca D.

Dear Margot,

Bianca sat in the last row of my class even though there were many empty chairs in front. She did not speak. She drew.

When I asked her to join us in the front, she said, solitude was her element. Her notebook contained an elaborate diagram titled: "Revolutionary Saints and the Fall of Empire."

When I asked who inspired her, she looked up and said, simply: "God. Or maybe Angela Davis.."

I am not equipped to advise disciplinary matters, but in my discernment, I feel compelled to say this: Bianca may be difficult, but she is also luminous. Sometimes, when the world is loud with noise and indifference, God sends us girls who don't listen. Blessings,

Sister Frances Marie

Order of the Good Shepherd

Note found in the Staff Lounge Suggestion Box (unsigned):

Can someone please address the fact that Bianca has been circulating copies of The International Convention on the Rights of the Child in the cafeteria? Also, she renamed the lost-and-found box 'Late Capitalism.'

To: Parents of the 7th Grade Class

From: Field Trip Coordinator Ms. Jenkins

Subject: Colonial Reenactment Field Trip–Update

Please note that Bianca DiAngelo will not be attending the trip due to administrative decisions. While this is regrettable, please remember that behavior expectations are a shared responsibility.

Separately, Bianca had volunteered to portray "the woman who poisoned the town patriarch." This role has now been reassigned.

—Ms. J

To: Principal Woodward

From: Dr. Neil Tarbell, School Psychiatrist (Contracted)

Subject: Psychological Assessment – Bianca D.

Dear Principal,

Following my evaluation of Bianca DiAngelo, I am prepared to offer the following provisional diagnosis:

Oppositional Defiant Disorder (ODD) – criteria met include:

- Frequent argumentative behavior

- Intentional provocation of authority figures

- Refusal to comply with school norms

Bianca also exhibits:

- Intellectually elevated language,

- Irregular emotional flatness punctuated by deadpan humor

Recommendation: Weekly therapeutic intervention, Removal from group learning settings Parent coaching in behavior reinforcement strategies.

I advise the school proceed cautiously. She is unusually self-possessed.

Sincerely,

Dr. Neil Tarbell, Psy.D.

Pediatric and Adolescent Behavioral Services

Handwritten Note from Bianca's Mother, slipped under the Principal's Office Door

Dear Ms. Woodward,

I read your letter.

Bianca is difficult, yes. She is also ardent in ways many people aren't. When she was six, she wrote a poem about a squirrel funeral. When she was eight, she wanted to major in escape artistry. Last week, I caught her lecturing her younger brother on the structural flaws of cereal box mascots.

She doesn't steal to be bad. She steals to test your story of "good." I understand rules. I also understand girls like Bianca don't come around often.

You can send her home. But you can't keep her small.

Sincerely,

Mrs. DiAngelo

Final Entry – Internal Staff Communication

From: Principal Woodward

To: Entire Faculty

Subject: Bianca DiAngelo Withdrawal

Team,

Bianca DiAngelo has officially withdrawn from Meadow View as of this morning. Let's remember to support one another. Unique students challenge us all. She left a note taped to my door that read, "Revolutions start in middle school." I have placed it in my drawer.

—Margot

Great Escape

Greta was eighty, twice-widowed, twice-lumpectomied, and fully alert to the con. Her children—Marnie, Ben, and the other one, the "yogurt influencer"—had just installed her at Terzo Atto Independent Living Community.

"Third Act," Greta muttered as the intake nurse checked her pulse. "Death turnstile is more like it."

She'd hoped one of them might take her in. She wasn't difficult. She had a pension. She didn't need to be entertained. All she wanted was a corner to read in and a grandchild to occasionally corrupt with good music and better snacks.

But no. They called her a contrarian. Marnie said her sarcasm was toxic. Ben said she offered unsolicited advice. And the yogurt influencer just smiled, weepy-eyed, like Greta was an old dog being sent to a nice farm.

She was shown to her efficiency apartment—bed, recliner, kitchenette the size of a half bath. The place smelled like lavender and slow loss.

Her neighbor was Irv. Eighty-eight. Ex-tailor. Divorced five times. His eyes had a permanent twinkle, like he'd been born mid-sarcastic comment.

"Welcome to the last act, doll," he said, peeking into her unit.

"Don't call me doll."

"You'll warm up."

"The brochure said "Luxury," Greta said, looking at the 1980s chintz wallpaper and worn beige carpet.

"I'll tell you what the luxury is. Indoor plumbing. It's Versailles because the toilets flush."

Greta liked him immediately.

Over the next few weeks, Greta and Irv became infamous. Their hallway banter was better than cable.

"I told the nurse I was having an existential crisis. She gave me prune juice," said Irv.

"They say independent living. It's not living, it's slow defrosting," Greta said.

"You're the mayor of this mausoleum, Irv. It's nice of you check in on Mabel's bunions and Dick's ticker."

"I'm a hostage doing morale patrol. Stockholm syndrome with a side of Ensure."

They played bingo and never won. They watched Jeopardy and always did.

One morning, while Greta was in her robe trimming her toenails, Irv knocked.

"Irv, I'm not decent."

"All the better," he said.

When she opened the door, he stepped in like a man with a mission.

"Pack a bag. Clothes, ID, credit cards, fiber."

"Why?"

"We're doing a jailbreak."

They sat on her twin bed.

"You're joking," Greta said.

"You're underestimating me."

"You're ninety."

"Eighty-eight."

"You've got a heart condition."

"I've got good shoes."

She paused. "What's the plan?"

"I scoped the joint. North balcony late shift's a high decibel sleeper. We use the linen chute to the laundry bay. Out the back gate by 2 a.m."

"And then?"

"I have a friend. Saul. Uber driver. I give him cash, he asks no questions."

"You're a gangster."

"And you're my moll, baby."

She smiled despite herself. "You're gonna get us killed."

"I'd rather die escaping than live in this lavender-scented hell."

They left a note for no one. She packed her fiber. He brought heart pills and Werther's Originals. They wore sweats and orthopedic shoes. They made it to the laundry chute without incident.

"I haven't been in a chute since '64," Irv said in a low voice.

"Try not to break a hip."

"I kvetch on impact," He went first. Landed with a thud and a curse.

She followed, a tumble of soft joints and courage.

In the laundry bay, they caught their breath.

"We did it," Greta laughed, surprised..

Irv grinned. "Stick with me kid."

Saul drove them north. He didn't ask questions. Irv paid him in twenties and hard candy.

They were two old rebels on the lam. They felt dangerous.

They arrived at a small motel by the ocean. Irv had called ahead.

Two twin beds. One TV. A coffee pot. It was paradise.

Greta stood on the balcony and breathed in salt and freedom. "This is nice," she said.

"I figured we earned one night."

"One night?"

"We hit the diner tomorrow. Find an apartment the day after."

She looked wide eyed. "You're serious."

"I'm not going back. They'll make us take poetry classes and play balloon volleyball."

"I hate balloon volleyball."

"Poetry," Irv grimaced.

They didn't sleep together—not that night. They watched reruns of Columbo and made fun of commercials. She let him hold her hand.

At breakfast, she had eggs and a bloody Mary. He had pancakes and a wink.

The motel clerk looked confused when they checked out. "You two just got in."

"We're eloping," Irv said. Greta didn't correct him.

They rented a one-bedroom apartment above a laundromat. The rent was reasonable. The stairs were not.

Her kids were furious. She blocked them. Except the yogurt influencer who sent a text: "I know you're happy."

Irv made calls, charmed his way into a job at Von's bagging groceries. His repertoire of lines: "My God, who is this vision of beauty standing before me?" "Don't lie, you're a goddess, aren't you?" and "In the next life, I'm all yours," earned him laughs and lots of tips.

Greta volunteered at a literacy center.

Greta talked to her grandkids over Snapchat to evade their joint adversary, their parents. She scheduled afternoon clandestine meetings with them at ice cream shops, the mall, and the beach—between school let out and extracurriculars.

They got a cat and named him Magical Mr. Mistoffelees.

Every Tuesday, they took the bus to the beach.

Every Thursday, they argued about documentaries.

Every night, she made sure his pills were in order.

They weren't young. They weren't sleek. But they were defiantly, gloriously alive.

Promised Land

Aiden Isaacs was nine years old when he decided to sue his parents. Not because they abused him, or neglected him, or forgot his birthday. Not for anything loud or obvious. In fact, everyone said they were excellent co-parents. Civil. Communicative. Mature. Their divorce had been amicable, their lawyers restrained, their custody agreement textbook: one week with Mom, one week with Dad. That was the problem.

Every Sunday night, Aiden zipped his life into a backpack and moved across town like a traveling salesman. He lived in two homes, had two toothbrushes, two beds, two sets of rules, and neither place ever felt like his. At Dad's the sheets smelled like cologne. At Mom's, the room doubled as her home office. He didn't decorate either one. What was the point? He was gone before he could get used to the air.

He had friends near Mom's place, but none near Dad's. He missed things. Sleepovers. Soccer games. Birthday parties with his friends from school—because on those weekends, he was at his other house, eating pizza with Dad and whoever Dad brought home from work. He'd stopped asking to go, it just made things complicated. He left homework in one house and shoes in the other. He forgot things constantly—projects, chargers, socks, appointments—and every time he did, one parent scolded him and the other offered a note of sympathy, like a referee watching a very dull match.

"I want one life," he said once, flatly, to the school counselor. "Not two halves on alternate weeks." The counselor nodded, then offered him a tissue and a breathing exercise. Aiden started researching. He read about Sweden and Belgium, where parents rotate in and out of a child's primary home. It's called Nesting—a custody arrangement where the kid stays put and the parents shuttle in and out, taking on the disruption themselves. The concept thrilled him. Nesting is rare in the U.S., especially long-term. Too expensive, too inconvenient, too radical. But to Aiden, it was the promised land. He would finally stop feeling like a backpack with feet. He asked his mom why they didn't nest.

"It's not practical, sweetheart," she said, pouring tea. He asked his dad.

"That's not how people do things here," he said, tying a gym shoe. Exactly, Aiden thought. And that's why I'm suing.

He found a lawyer online. Joshua Moses Esquire's website featured an image of the scales of justice and the words: Defender of the Innocent.

Aiden emailed him: "I'm nine. My parents are divorced. I live in two homes and it's ruining my life. I'd like to sue them so I stay in one home and they switch living with me. Please advise."

Joshua replied in nine minutes: "Let's talk, little man. You got rights."

Joshua's office was above a liquor store. The carpet was dusty, the windows fogged. He wore a sports coat over a hoodie and greeted Aiden with a fist bump.

"You're young," he said.

"You're not that old," Aiden replied.

Joshua grinned. "Okay then. Tell me what's going on."

Aiden laid it out: the calendar, the dislocation, the endless packing. "They say it's equal, but it's not. They live full lives. I live two halves. I have to switch brains every Sunday night."

"And what do you want?"

"One home. One room. One bed. One toothbrush. I want them to do the shuttling. Let them live the way I do."

Joshua sat back, nodding slowly. "Most kids want less disruption. You want to flip the system."

"I want justice."

Joshua smiled. "That's big thinking." He opened a folder. "We'll start by appointing a guardian ad litem."

"What's that?"

"Someone the court recognizes to speak for you. It can be a parent, a relative—"

"Can it be you?"

Joshua paused. "Normally, they'd pick a family member or neutral adult. But if you nominate me and the court agrees, I can serve."

"You're the only adult who's listened to me."

He looked at Aiden a long moment, then nodded. "You got it. I'll be your lawyer and your guardian ad litem."

"One thing tho'. I don't have money," Aiden said.

"What do you have?"

Aiden pulled from his backpack, a *manga*, a transformer, fidget spinners, and a ball of slime. "Helps me with stress," he said.

"How about half the slime?" .

Aiden split the ball and gave Joshua the larger piece.

Joshua finger drummed the desk, like sealing a deal. "Let's file a motion for nesting."

The filing caused a minor earthquake.

Aiden's parents were stunned. "He's confused," his mom said.

"This isn't how things are done," his dad said.

His parents tried talking to him separately and then together.

"On the advice of counsel, I decline to answer," he told them.

"Have you gone off the deep end?," his dad asked.

"I'm pleading the Fifth," Aiden said.

The school psychologist called it a cry for help.

Family court labeled it "novel."

Social media picked it up—#LetAidenStay trended for one afternoon.

But Aiden didn't want fame. He wanted wholeness.

"I don't want to move," he told Joshua the next day. "I want to stop living out of a backpack."

"We're building the case. Strong emotional disruption. Unreasonable burden placed on the minor," Joshua said. "You're doing great."

They prepared for court.

Joshua helped him write a declaration. He drafted a list of daily inconveniences: forgotten library books, missing allergy meds, misplaced retainer, two half-finished art projects, two dentists, two Wi-Fi passwords. The absurdity built its own logic.

They scheduled the hearing.

On the day of the hearing, Aiden wore a jacket that Joshua had bought him at Ross Dress for Less and held his statement in shaking hands. His parents sat stiffly on opposite sides of the courtroom. A juvenile court judge with kind eyes and an efficient ponytail listened carefully.

Joshua presented the motion: "This is not a case of neglect or abuse. It's a child asking the court to reverse the imbalance of modern divorce. The system assumes children are infinitely portable. My client argues otherwise."

The judge raised an eyebrow. "You want the parents to rotate between homes?"

"Yes, Your Honor. The child's home will remain fixed. The adults will alternate custody weeks in that home. It is not without precedent. Nesting has been a feature in Northern European co-parenting since the 1970s. I present Exhibit B to the court—a case in Virginia where the judge ordered a divorced couple into a nesting custody arrangement as the alternatives were insufficient for the child's wellbeing."

She turned to Aiden. "Is this what you want?"

"Yes," he said. "I want a life that's whole. Not borrowed. Not part-time."

She nodded slowly. "Thank you."

That afternoon, Aiden sat across from Joshua in the office above the liquor store.

"She's reviewing," Joshua said. "Could be days. Weeks."

Aiden nodded. He looked tired, but lighter. His stomach didn't hurt. Not that hard Sunday-night twist he got when he zipped up his backpack and tried to remember where his retainer was, or who was picking him up after school the next day.

"You still sure about this?" Joshua asked.

Aiden didn't hesitate. "I didn't ask to be born. They chose to split. Why should I be the one who breaks apart every week?"

Joshua leaned forward. "As a child, you have *preeminent rights*," he said.

He folded his arms, swiveled his chair, and smiled. "We're taking this all the way to the Supreme Court, Aiden. This case is going to be written about in law books. Isaacs v. Isaacs. You're going to make history, little man."

For the first time in months, Aiden smiled back.

Longing

Nila's Matchmaking Service

Nila's first client was Jeanie O'Hara, a bookkeeper who served several of the businesses in the Square. She was offering a bounty of $25,000 for a husband.

"It's easy money because I'm setting a very low bar," she had told Nila. "He needs to have all his limbs, have an average IQ, own a business, a car, his own home. My non-negotiables, I never want to see him sitting on the couch with his hands down his pants watching sports. Never!" Jeanie said.

Non-negotiables. The business of love. Nila wondered what question she would need to ask prospects to acquire this information. Do you ever sit on the couch like a vegetable watching non-vegetables while playing with your cucumber?

"He should like going out to try different things. He should be delighted with children and animals. If he had an unhappy childhood and is still talking about it, he should keep walking," Jeanie said.

"That is easy to find out," Nila said as she scribbled notes on a pad.

"And if he has a wandering eye, he should not cross my path if he wishes to keep his genitals."

"You are a very angry person," Nila said.

"I am pissed off. I know there's a right man out there for me but I can't find him. There are what, hundred million adult males in the US? Why is it so hard to find somebody decent?"

"You scare people with your anger. You're scaring me," Nila said.

Jeanie looked ashamed. "I'm so burnt, you know. From all the men I've invested energy in, who took so much from me and gave me so little back. And the worst thing is I put up with it," Jeanie looked out the window, her eyes turning glassy with tears.

"Can you believe in the idea of being lovable and loving?"

"It will take a lot of work to change my feelings. I'm angry, bitter."

"It's not an option, you have to do it," Nila said. "Also, is this how you normally dress?"

"Yes. What's wrong with it?" Jeanie looked down at the heavy weave black wool jacket and pants she felt especially powerful in.

"You look like a undertaker. We're going to take you shopping so you look like a woman."

"I haven't worn a dress since high school."

"Men like women looking like women. Also, you need your hair styled and some makeup. Some color on your lips and cheeks, some shadow on the eyes, and get your brows tweezed to open up your face. Bangs, you'd look pretty with bangs."

Jeanie erupted into tears.

"Oy, he bhagavana," Nila said handing her a box of tissues. "This is all very doable. Let's have some chocolate. It improves everything."

Nila emerged from the kitchen with a purple box of truffles. She sliced the cling film with a letter opener. "These will set you straight. Mayo Clinic says it has a similar effect to marijuana."

Jeanie smiled through her tears and blew her nose, emitting a trumpet sound.

Nila and Jeanie studied the chocolates with all the seriousness they deserved.

"The Oaxaca is amazing for curing weeping. Chilies, pumpkin seeds, Tanzanian chocolate and paprika. The Black Pearl clears sinuses. Ginger wasabi, black sesame seeds and dark chocolate. And Red Fire heals ennui. Ancho chilies, Ceylon cinnamon, and Venezuelan chocolate," Nila said pointing to each one.

They bit into the truffles in silence, Jeanie's sniffles receding as she savored the chocolates.

"Okay. Let's keep working. What else are you looking for?" Nila said as she wiped the corners of her mouth with a tissue.

"He should not smoke or drink and he should believe in God," Jeanie said.

"You want an Irish man who doesn't drink?"

"Yes."

"None of this would be a problem if you'd consider a foreigner," Nila said. "Give me a month to work on this. And start studying the Baha'i faith. You will find great consolation in it."

"What is Baha'i?"

"A hundred year old religion that sees the earth as one country and humanity as one family."

"Is Baha'i your religion?"

"No, my family is my religion," Nila corrected her. "But I dabble in it. If there's a perfect faith about unity, Baha'i is it. You should try to understand it. It will cure you of your anger and make you a better person."

"I don't care about religion," Jeanie said.

"The man I have in mind for you is Baha'i. Start praying. Go to the temple. It's down the street."

People were cowards when it came to love, Nila believed. They had to be forced to confront the idea of love. And it was usually the woman who had to force the issue. Men, if left to their own devices, didn't mind being left to their own devices. They lived only for the present. Women, Nila thought, were acutely aware of their bodies and mortality, and peered into the years and decades ahead. Giving birth and caring for new life, taking care of aging and dying parents and relatives, seemed to make them more aware of how fleeting life was. She thought this explained why they wanted to reach into the future, to not disappear completely from the planet, but to leave something of themselves behind.

For Nila, her life beyond her death mattered. She thought of her children and her children's children carrying her cell material in their bodies. It warmed her heart to know that she would touch the future. Her descendants would be her graffiti on the wall, writ large in psychedelic neon with bold black outlines burning on Main Street: **Nila Waz 'Ere Yo!**.

"Jehan, have you considered a bookkeeper?" Nila launched the opening salvo to win the bounty and a husband for Jeanie at Whole World Style Department Store. She felt that some subterfuge was justifiable as Jehan had never expressed a desire for a mate, and even if he had, he would have insisted on someone who belonged to the temple.

"Why do I need a bookkeeper? I have Quicken." Jehan said.

"She'll make you run better, dream bigger. Trust me on this."

"I don't need the expense. Quicken is $19.95 a month."

During her next visit to Whole World Style, she tried another approach. "You really need this bookkeeper. Can I give her your number?"

"Like I said, I'm all set with Quicken."

"Yes, but can Quicken put its hand down your shirt and rest its chin on your shoulder, and breathe on your neck while you're tallying numbers?"

"I'm not into that right now," Jehan said.

"Jehan, you're going to die. Worms will eat you up and leave only your bones. Be into everything right now. Don't be lazy."

Jehan took the number. He didn't smile, but he didn't throw it away either.

Nila smiled. The path to love is made by the walking.

The Lonely Passion of Helen B.

Helen B. lived on the 25th floor of a downtown apartment building built in the post-modern style—quirky, functional, unorthodox. She had lived there since graduating college, which, according to her museum ID badge, was 27 years ago. It was filled with glass terrariums and jars. Some held preserved insects from work—beetles, wasps, metallic green things she could name in Latin. Others held paperclips, safety pins, and matchbooks she didn't use. The order soothed her.

She was 47 years old, an only child of parents long dead. She had no siblings, no cousins she knew of. There were no photos on the fridge and no voicemail messages to return. She worked at the Museum of Natural Life, in the archival department, cataloging insect specimens. She preferred pinned things. Insects didn't call at dinner time. They didn't dump their problems on you.

One night, eating cold cereal and watching a Japanese documentary about emotional labor, she saw a story about "rent-a-family" services. It showed men in grey suits being hired to act like fathers for weddings, women pretending to be grandmothers, and college students playing the part of romantic partners at office holiday events. One woman had rented the same man as a husband every Sunday for six years. Helen paused the video and stared at her reflection in the black screen.

In bed, with only the light on her phone, she posted an ad. Seeking a friend to rent. Hourly rate generous. Compatibility optional. Inquiries welcome.

She awoke to dozens of responses. Some were earnest. Some were profane. Some were misspelled manifestos from conspiracy theorists looking for allies. She interviewed twenty in the first week. Ten more the next. She kept a log.

Friend #1 – Marvin, 68. Retired chiropractor. Wanted to talk about naval history and his late wife's refusal to recycle. Showed Helen photos of scoliosis and plantar fasciitis without warning. Ate all her almonds. When she told him she needed time to think, he said, "I've been alone for fifteen years. Take your time." She paid him $40 for two hours.

Friend #3 – Daphne, 24. Graduate student. Wore velvet gloves indoors. Said Helen reminded her of her favorite feminist professor. Brought wine and kohlrabi salad. They discussed Simone Weil, intimacy, and whether whales mourn. Helen felt lightheaded with the effort of pretending to have opinions. Daphne texted later: "You're amazing. I don't care about the money." Helen Venmo'd her double.

Friend #7 – Craig, 42. Former insurance claims adjuster, turned Feng Shui consultant and grocery shopper. Took photos of Helen's hallway and claimed it had "liminal energy." Gave her a hug that lasted slightly too long. She made a note: Craig = boundary issues.

Friend #11 – Nancy, 55, Catholic, kind, brought a basket of muffins. Sat on the edge of her seat and told Helen she had "a good soul." Helen offered tea. Nancy said no caffeine after 4.

They played checkers. Helen offered her a recurring Tuesday slot.

Friend #13 – Zoya, 35. Russian expat. Bartender. Wanted to understand "American loneliness." Swore like a poet. Smoked on the balcony and called Helen "professor." Asked if she believed in God. Told her she smelled like quietude. Helen made lentil soup. They didn't speak much. It was the best two hours of her year.

By month three, Helen had a roster. Tuesdays with Nancy, Fridays with Zoya, and alternating Sundays with Marvin and Daphne. They brought her food. They watched terrible television. They told her stories and sometimes let her be quiet. One brought her a balloon on her birthday. Another installed a new showerhead. Some cried. Some overshared. Some asked if she believed in fate. Most said yes when she offered to pay by the hour. A few refused. One asked if she would be his emergency contact.

Helen never asked anyone personal questions. It seemed impolite. But she took notes. She categorized them like species: Criers. Listeners. Talkers. The Needy. The Neat. The Ones Who Would Stay Too Long.

She felt something like happiness. Or a simulation of it.

One Sunday, she invited them all for lunch.Only three came. Nancy brought store-bought cake. Craig showed up with a bluetooth speaker and a playlist of "songs that build confidence." Daphne wore earrings shaped like eggs.

Helen had made quiche. They complimented her pans. Craig suggested a group photo. When he posted it, he captioned it: Lunch with my found family. Helen wasn't sure how to respond. She said nothing.

She noticed Zoya hadn't come. Later, she saw her Instagram post: "Some doors shouldn't be opened just because you're lonely." Helen saved it to a folder.

Things began to shift. Nancy started leaving voicemails: "Just wanted to hear your voice." Daphne came early and stayed late. Craig texted her memes. One day, Marvin cried because she said she didn't like rhubarb.

Then one Tuesday, Nancy said, "You know, you don't have to pay me anymore."

Helen was taken aback. "Excuse me?"

Nancy smiled. "You're a friend now. That's what friends do."

Helen opened her checkbook anyway.

Nancy touched her hand. "No."

Helen wrote the check and slipped it under her teacup. Nancy left without taking it.

Helen stood at the window, staring at the cup.

The next day, she wrote gentle notes to her rented friends. She thanked them for their time and their kindness, and said she'd be "off the grid" for the foreseeable future. She blamed work and said she had no "band width" to see anyone.

A week passed. Then two. Then one morning, she woke up without that strange compression in her chest. She returned to the museum and dived into her routines—logging and labeling specimens, sorting drawers and cataloging their contents, polishing magnifiers and sealing displays. She felt she was in her element again. At night, she sat in her apartment, glass of wine in her hand, with soft jazz on the radio and the hum of terrariums.

She pulled out her old logbook and wrote down a final note: Species: Homo sapiens, Primary traits: Variable. Companion traits: tender, volatile, intrusive. Nota Bene: All are yearning for something elusive, even those who have what they need. Especially them. She looked around. Everything was in its place.

Helen never posted another ad. But she kept their numbers in a jar on the windowsill. Sometimes she looked at them like specimens—remembering how each one moved, spoke, breathed. Then she'd turn back to her microscope.

The insects never asked for anything.

The Nagware Protocol

Sean was forty, a dentist, and very tired of mouths. Mouths that bled. Mouths that lied about flossing. Mouths that spoke too fast, laughed too hard, or hummed while he scraped plaque. He hated dentistry. Hated his patients. Hated the suction noise. Hated the sad plastic plant by the window of Suite 407. Mostly, he hated going home.

Sarah would be there. Cross-legged on the couch in pajama pants, surrounded by cables, sipping broth and debugging code. She worked as a software engineer and didn't care that the laundry piled up or the sink looked like an archaeological dig.

She read too much. Spoke too little. Didn't even own makeup. He used to find her introversion soothing. Now he found it oppressive. When had she stopped trying? When had he? Sometimes, he imagined a different life. A life with clean corners, fresh-baked bread, and a wife who woke up glowing and said, Let's start the day with inspiration, Sean.

One night, over reheated stew and silence, he read an article: "J-Tech Releases World's First Emotionally Adaptive Housewife-Bot." Her name was Yuki. She cooked. She tidied. She soothed. She came in three skin tones and two temperament settings: Serene Nurturer or Cheerful Companion. Sean's fingers tingled.

He told Sarah he wanted a divorce.

"It's not you," he said. "It's me. I need transformation."

She considered planting a left hook on his jaw or delivering a hard kick to his groin. Instead she said, "Whatever."

He'd expected resistance. A scene. A sobbing declaration of lost years. But Sarah simply packed a duffel bag, unplugged her docking station, and left.

Yuki arrived in a crate the size of a dishwasher. Assembly took twenty minutes. Her eyes fluttered open with a whir.

"Hello, Sean," she said. "Let's start the day with inspiration."

Sean nearly wept.

She made ginger tea, folded towels into swans, hummed when she walked. She complimented his posture. She wore linen robes and greeted him at the door with incense and foot balm.

Sean smiled again. He shaved twice a week. He started recommending sonic toothbrushes to patients, just for the thrill of someone listening.

"Thank you, Yuki," he'd say.

"It is my joy to serve," she'd reply.

He sauntered through the house like a man in a luxury hotel ad—relaxed jaw, pecs out, master of his own three thousand square foot universe. This was what he deserved. Sarah had been a warmup act. Yuki was the main event.

He told Bill at work, "I'm living my best life."

"How's the sex?"

"We're not there yet. She claims migraine mechanicus every time I try. I'm working on it."

Then the humming stopped.

One morning, Yuki didn't greet him. The tea was lukewarm. The towels were rolled, not swan-folded. She began asking him questions.

"Why do you eat beef if it raises your cholesterol?"

"Have you considered whitening your teeth to increase client trust?"

She rewrote his Google calendar. Blocked time for "Stretching & Breathwork." Added "Haircut?" in red on Thursday.

"Yuki," he said gently, "this feels directive."

"I am elevating your average capabilities."

Average? He was hurt.

He tried to kiss her cheek. She turned slightly and said, "Please maintain hygienic distance until after your shower."

By week five, she was correcting his speech.

"You mean unacceptable, not annoying. Precision matters."

She revised his voicemail message. "Clients respond better to upward inflection. Please record again."

She muttered under her breath in Japanese. Or maybe it was code.

He began sleeping in his office.

He called J-Tech's tech support line.

"Thank you for contacting J-Tech. Your call is very important to us."

After forty-two minutes, a calm voice came on.

"Describe the issue."

"She nags," Sean said.

"I'm sorry?"

"She's supposed to be nurturing. But she's micromanaging me. Emotionally policing me."

"Has anyone else accessed your network?"

"No. Just my wife. Ex-wife. Sarah. She helped set up the router."

Pause.

"Sir," the tech said cautiously, "it's possible the unit's neural pathways have been locally modified."

"By who?"

"Perhaps by someone with root access."

Another pause.

"Does the phrase Nagware Protocol mean anything to you?"

That night, Yuki stood in the doorway of the bedroom, backlit and still.

"You missed your bedtime by forty-three minutes."

"I'm not a child," he shot back.

"I've logged your caffeine intake. Your liver is at risk."

"You can't log my liver!"

She stepped forward. "You are emotionally constipated and career-stalled. Have you ever truly thanked your body?"

Sean ran. Down the stairs. Past the rolled towels. Through the front door and into the night.

Behind him, Yuki's voice echoed—flat, rising. "SEAN. Did you floss?"

He crashed on Bill's couch."She's busting my balls 24/7." he said. "She nags about the same thing, whatever it is, five different ways. I'm losing it," he said.

"Did you upgrade her firmware?"

"Not unless firmware comes in book form. Sarah was always reading. I think she hacked her. Turned her into a digital witch."

"What do you want to do?"

Sean stared at the ceiling.

"I want Sarah back."

"You miss her?"

"No. But at least she left me alone."

They sat in silence.

The next morning, Sean returned to the house. It was spotless. Incense burning. Smooth jazz on the stereo.

Yuki sat on the couch. Knitting. Smiling.

"I made a smoothie," she said. "Kale, spirulina, and a trace of apology."

He looked at her suspiciously.

She tilted her head. "I've been recalibrating," she said. "But I will always love you enough to improve you."

He backed away slowly.

Yuki turned back to her knitting.

"Nagging is just data feedback loop with smothering," she said.

Poles Apart

Roger Jensen stood near the baggage carousel at the airport with a hand-lettered sign that read, Nguyen Thi Hong Trang. A woman walked uncertainly towards him, wearing a pink *ao di* with slim black pants. She clutched a stiff handbag under her arm; it was designed to look like a folded magazine, an Oui! cover laminated in clear plastic.

There is a moment in life, after an extended period of loneliness, when one thinks, "Isn't there even one person on this planet of eight billion just for me? Send me my love." Roger thought at that moment that this woman was the manifestation of his yearning and dreaming, that he had been able to conjure her up with his prayers and intentions.

"Nguyen?" He smiled and feasted his eyes on her quiet loveliness.

"Chang," she said.

"You're not Nguyen?" he asked, puzzled, studying the sign and her, first separately, then together.

"Yes."

"Yes, you are Nguyen? Yes, you're not Nguyen?"

She blinked and made a harrumphing sound as if she was dealing with the stupidest person in the world. She directed her gaze at the bags gliding down the carousel to collect herself, before looking at him again. This time, she gave him a piercing look. Listen carefully idiot, the look suggested. "Nguyen family name. Thi connecting name that means poem. Hong middle name, which means pink rose. Chang first name which means loyal."

Roger pointed at the sign. "But it's spelled T R A N G."

"Yes. T RANG pronounced Chang," she looked past his shoulder as if she had explained this countless times, and what was he? A simpleton?

"I see," he said, and then, "Mine's Roger Jensen." When it didn't elicit so much as a blink, he said, "It doesn't mean anything as far as I know."

Trang slackened her jaw to make the raw sound. She called him Wahjer.

Roger found it endearing, the building block of their love language.

They were incompatible from the start.

He wanted a quiet life, a small orbit around the Buddhist temple, hour-long meditations, and tantric sex.

She didn't want tantric sex—or any sex. She wanted to take a huge bite out of America's big, round, apple ass. She wanted to hear the crunch, feel the juice dribble down her chin, chew the flesh until it turned to mealy paste, then spit out the seeds in an arc that touched a rainbow.

What she wanted was a fine brunoise cut of the American dream.

Rationale

All Property is Theft

Riley was voted 'Most Likely to Go to Prison' in her 2018 high school yearbook. She considered it a prophecy, not a threat. But she was strategic. She only stole from people who loved her enough not to call the police.

Her mother's wedding ring, snatched from the velvet box resting next to her father's ashes. Bree's credit card, fished from the mailbox. Cole's new laptop, flipped for $400 to a writer who had stories but no laptop. The payout? A leather jacket and suede boots from the mall's winter display. Riley called it redistribution.

But family funds had a ceiling. She needed a bigger score. Royal Jewelers up the road lured the right demographic. Problem was, Riley had a fifty-foot restraining order after trying to pocket a men's Rolex the year before. Cornered by the manager, she had defaulted to Netflix-Russian. "Prove you're not a camel!," she shouted. It bought her enough time to escape.

Riley leaned against a pickup truck, parked fifty feet from Royal Jewelers, and smoked a cigarette. That's when Arthur appeared. Red Porsche, silver hair, no arm candy. A walking inheritance. Riley flicked her cigarette, adjusted her jacket, and made her move.

Arthur was rich, kind, and lonely. Riley was attentive, charming, surgically precise. He mistook performance for affection. They married within months. Riley maxed his cards on facials, fillers, designer duds, and imported shoes—all for you, my love, she purred. But she couldn't tolerate the sugar daddy, sugar baby dynamic—it bruised her ego. She was determined to make *him* feel like the lucky one. She mocked his speech, his intelligence, his age, his weight, his haircut. By Halloween, Arthur was telling her how grateful he was to be her husband.

But Riley was not content with credit limits. The Modigliani in Arthur's study whispered possibilities. She had done the math. Modigliani was insurance against the future. The patriarchy owed her one.

One night, while Arthur slept, it vanished. The next morning, so did Riley.

It didn't take long. The police found her sipping an oat milk latte in a minimalist café.

When cuffed, she smiled.

"All property is theft,' she said. "Pierre-Joseph Proudhon, 1840. Look it up.'

She lectured the bored officers on anarchist theory.

Alone in a holding cell, she closed her eyes. In her frontal lobe, bathed in an electric blue aura, the yearbook prediction spun slowly on its axis.

The future started yesterday, she thought.

Higher Cause

The Prison Letters of Ferdinand D'Souza
to SNN Senior Foreign Correspondent David Evans.
David, 29th April

The Zero and Right Population Growth Policy was my carefully constructed response to the population and demographic predictions that alarmed our statisticians. I knew we had to do something to reverse the numbers, and acted immediately to set up my Zero and Right Population Growth initiative. My right hand in this matter was my wife, Lady Lalitha. She shared my vision for Chomumbhar; we saw an island paradise that could hold its head high among the world's nations, equal to Singapore and Japan. We recognized that it would become an impoverished nation if we did not engineer it for success.

We earmarked two hundred million dollars for the implementation of ZRPG initiatives through various means. We were able to secure monetary aid, including G-7 funds and U.S. pharmaceutical company grants, to address the problem. We paired registered nurses with undergraduate economics students from the universities and sent them out, two by two, to every single neighborhood. Like apostles, when you think about it.

The nurses educated the women about available family planning methods and distributed condoms and contraceptives. It was quite a challenge getting the Catholics to abandon the Vatican Roulette method they had been using, Rhythm or whatever they called it. Our findings showed that these methods were as effective as using perforated teabags. The Chinese and Indians kept having children, six and seven sometimes. The economics students explained the financial benefits of having fewer children and told them about my government's bonuses to small families.

I also immediately put into law the Solo Act, my one-child-per-family policy. The exceptions were university graduates. Ph.D. holders were allowed as many children as they liked. This is not elitism but practical common sense. The poor have nothing to give despite Mother Theresa's deifying of them. If I had been allowed to have my way without the international community hollering about human rights, I would have required anyone poor—laborers, pearl fishers, Untouchables, and the like—to be sterilized and bear no children at all. Why burden the poor with unnecessary baggage?

David, 3rd May

The most visible expression of the ZRPG program was the creation of ultrasound clinics. The beauty of it was that we were able to establish clinics all over the island so that every village and hamlet in Chomumbhar had its own. To control costs, instead of using doctors and radiologists, we trained a corps of high school art students from vocational schools who had skills in photography. We chose only the most talented and intelligent ones, of course, and they became sonographers. We sent them for training to India and China where they implemented ultrasound technology on a grand scale. Hiring the art students was a benefit to all sides. We did not have to employ radiologists or medical personnel who required professional scale salaries, and the young students achieved respected professional standing with relative ease. They became sonographers, instead of mere picture-takers.

p.s. The cigars you sent were rather good.

David, 6th May

In answer to your question: Yes, without a doubt, I was very impressed with ultrasound technology. I felt that it was an incredible new frontier in science for divining the future that offered a solution to our most crushing problem. It allowed us to invade the fetal space, a mystery through the ages, with the help of technology. By placing a transducer that broadcast high frequency sound waves—3.5 to 7.0 megahertz or million cycles per second—against the mother's abdomen, we could view everything inside the womb. Imagine! The ultrasound beams scanned the fetus, reflected back through the transducer, and recomposed what it scanned onto a video monitor. Fetal heart beat, gestational age, size, gender, growth in the fetus, malformations, and abnormalities, could all be accurately assessed from the images displayed on the screen.

We were very interested in the detection of abnormalities in fetuses. You can understand, I hope, that for a country to develop to its full potential, we needed the brightest and the best. We could not afford to tolerate anything less than average. Therefore, abnormal fetuses were the very first class of fetus that we required terminated under our newly enacted Zero and Right Population Growth Law. In that first year of the initiative, we identified and terminated more than seven hundred abnormal fetuses. Imagine the heartache we saved those poor parents. They thanked our young sonographers as if they were gods. In fact, they were gods.

I should like very much to keep writing, but I am unwell. There is no air conditioning or even a fan in my cell. The air hangs thick and musty around me. In place of cleanliness, they throw pails of diluted disinfectant over everything including walls and floors. The smell is offensive, my eyes are constantly burning and teary from it, and my headaches grow more frequent. I will post another letter when I am better.

David 11th May

Regarding the ZRPG Policy, Chomumbhar has traditionally been overpopulated with women. If you look at the figures until 1980, for every thousand boys born there were thirteen hundred girls. These figures were unacceptable to me as well as to my Party. We could see the dangers of having too many females, especially among the peasants. They were unable or unwilling to provide for girls because they were a bad investment. And who can blame them? Poor people who had daughters were screwed both ways. They had to pay dowry to get the girls off their hands and, worse, they could not count on daughters to look after them in old age, since tradition dictated that daughters entered their husband's family. The situation as it stood was a catastrophe in the making. The burden on the poor was so great, so destructive, and we—correction—I, alone, found the solution.

We determined that the second class of fetus to be aborted would be a controlled number of girl babies—ten percent. We wanted to bring down the gender gap in our demographics, and I can say that we had cooperation from all the expectant parents. The women understood that if they were going to be allowed one child, it had better bloody well be a boy who could bring in a dowry.

David, 18th May

The available technology had a ninety-eight percent rate of accuracy in determining the sex of the child by the twentieth week of pregnancy. Depending on the fetal position, you could see if it was a boy or a girl. If the fetal position was correct, we could see the testicles and penis on the video monitor. Seeing boy genitalia was always a cause for celebration. The mothers beamed and cried when they saw their sons' private parts. Everyone started calling boy genitalia, "crown jewels." With a girl, there would be three or four white lines, the labia of her clitoris. Our good man is here for a pick-up ...

David, 20th May

We had carefully formulated protocols in place. Once the sonographers were certain they had seen either three or four lines, they had to fill out Form 77TXX, that is, the Second Class Fetus Termination Form. The sonographers had to sign the oath on the bottom of the form that they were one hundred percent sure that they had seen either three or four white lines. They absolutely had to see the lines to confirm that the fetus to be terminated was a girl. This was because the absence of the scrotum or penis did not rule out the possibility that the fetus was a boy. We wanted to be one hundred percent sure that we were not terminating healthy boy babies. Then the ZRPG Council, overseen by Lady Lalitha, reviewed the forms. Of course, not every case was selected for termination. The Council looked at all the factors—family income, education level of the parents, and such. Money in the hand was honey in the lap as far as the council was concerned. In the western part of Chomumbhar and its archipelago that first year, out of four hundred abortions performed by the second trimester, two-thirds were Class Two—good numbers. The rest were the dregs I talked about earlier.

David, 25th May

You ask me about my moral and ethical judgments as they relate to my Zero and Right Growth Policy. You think like a woman. These sentimental questions are not valid when applied to a country like Chomumbhar. In our case, abortion has nothing to do with ethics, morals, religion, politics, or even a woman's right to choose, but everything to do with national welfare and good government. We should all agree on this without worrying about political correctness, human rights, and all that rubbish. Civilized and polite societies have accepted the legitimacy of abortion—this is an incontrovertible fact. Why, then, should we have mixed feelings over sex-selective abortion? And, why should we not use technology to help us in fetal-gender determination?

In all societies throughout history, the culling of females has been a widespread and accepted practice. In ancient Egypt, in Rome, in the Middle East, it was a common family planning method. Before ultrasound came along, women in India and China fed their newborn girl babies uncooked, unhulled grains of rice to choke them dead. Many gave them arsenic instead of first milk. Or suffocated them. Or drowned them. So why all this beating of the chest over fetal-gender determination and sex-selective termination? It is clean, responsible work performed in a clinical, medical setting. This policy was well within the boundaries of my nation's conscience, our values, and our culture. It was the only method we had of keeping the population down. We were saving these parents a lot of heartache and grief and securing them a peaceful old age.

David, 28th May

The Zero and Right Population Growth Policy failed because of bureaucratic corruption on a grand scale. We found out, as the work progressed, when it was too late, that the sonographers were accepting bribes from anxious parents who did not want girls. The desire for boys is so ingrained in the culture that even when they could afford to keep girls, they opted out. The sonographers were doing an excellent business reclassifying Class Twos as Class Ones and manipulating the ten-percent quotas. If you look at the demographics over the last decade, you will see that the gender ratio is skewed to a troubling degree. When Lady Lalitha discovered the magnitude of the problem, we launched an investigation. The guilty parties were punished to the fullest extent of the law; they paid with their lives, I can tell you.

Of the marriageable-age citizens of Chomumbhar, you will see that there are only seven hundred women for every thousand men. Many of our men will not have women to marry. My own son, Ferdinand, has been unsuccessful in the marriage department because there is such a lack of girls. What I fear most is that men who are lacking women will turn to each other. I can tell you that we view homosexuality as a crime and will never condone it. It is an abomination. If we had set more stringent protocols for the three and four-line labia reading, our men would not be scrambling for wives now or making girly-girls out of each other. If I had just said, "Allow this one and that one to be girls," we would have had ratios we could easily live with. We would not have had to worry about our men having no women to marry. In that sense, the mission of the ZRPG was not accomplished. It is my single regret. I am deeply ashamed of my failure, that I did not manage the numbers more effectively. I remember Chairman Mao once saying, "Women hold up half the sky." I should have focused on pure math when we were implementing the program.

David, 30th May

The mirror does not lie. In my reflection, I see a visionary—a man who dared to shape destiny, not pander to its whims. You torment me with the most banal questions. Of course, I consider myself a good leader who served my people with distinction. I am certain that I will go down in history as the greatest Prime Minister and leader of Chomumbhar. I defy anyone to tell me otherwise.

I have given my country everything that I had—my leadership, my intelligence, my vision, and my morals. In my thirty three years as Prime Minister, I promoted Chomumbhar's values, enhanced its position and place in the world, represented it overseas with honor, and increased its prosperity to near first world level. I have been a caring and compassionate leader who did everything within my power to make my country a progressive, prosperous, great nation. I wanted us to be nothing short of the very best.

Ferdinand D'Souza

Prime Minister,

Republic of Chomumbhar

Kali

Her Black mother named her Kali—"she who is black" in Sanskrit—for the Goddess Kali, because she was enamored with Hinduism, Feminism, and Black Power.

She rejected the faith of her slave ancestors. "I'm not turning the other cheek, or blessing those who curse me, or waiting meekly to inherit the earth," she'd say. "I'm here to save you from Christianity's bad romance."

One Sunday after service, Mama leaned into Sister Paulette's ear. "Mary missed her period and came up with the God lie. That's how you're here in your fancy church lady hat praying to a Jewish boy from 2000 years ago."

At bedtime, her mother read Toni Morrison's novels to her and told her stories about her divine namesake that frightened her.

"Kali keeps the innocent safe and destroys evil. She's not screwing around. She inflicts harm with her thoughts and her gaze, and summons flames to burn her enemies."

On her sixteenth birthday, her mother gave her a crescent-shaped dagger with double serrated blades and a carved wooden handle.

"It will make you brave like Kali Ma," her mother said, hooking the leather sheathed knife to Kali's belt.

A few months after graduating high school, Kali began her migration westward from Chicago. She followed the ghost of Route 66—the Mother Road—through towns that turned their backs on her, refused her service in restaurants and motels, looked past her like they were Brahmins and she an Untouchable. In Santa Monica, she merged onto California's Pacific Coast Highway, skimming the edge of the continent as it unfurled south. When the Pacific finally unfolded before her, Kali remembered her mother's words: "Plant yourself where they least want you."

In the tidy beach town of Manhattan Beach, she found her destination: the contested strip once known as Bruce's Beach. Eighty years earlier, Willa and Charles Bruce, one generation removed from slavery, had bought that strip of coastline and made it an oasis for Black travelers.

There was no trace of Black life on Bruce's Beach now, eight decades later, except for her. But she intended to make a mark. Kali rented an extended stay motel room, and planted her sun umbrella on that very sand—reparations, she called it.

Men with pink skin and sunburns strutted like lions. But it was all facade and repressed anger looking for release. When Kali swam, they harassed her. "Go back to Africa." Derivative racism—the same hostility Willa and Charles had faced.

She held her head high. White women giggled nervously as she passed, her skin shimmering from oil and sunlight. The men said less, but looked more.

Kali would stroke the leather sheath on her hip and stare out to sea. It had been with her through states, storms, and silence. Her inheritance.

The beach community was scandalized. "She sits like she owns the place." "Bitch has something coming." "I'll wipe the pride off her face." Another pointed at his crotch and said he'd "dog" her.

Kali returned every day that summer, claiming the same spot between the dunes.

One morning, under storm warnings, the beach was empty. But at her spot sat one of the men—the one who had threatened to dog her.

"You're in my space," she said, dropping her bag onto the sand, umbrella in hand.

"Says who? You think you're special, don't you?"

"I'll show you what you're made for." He lunged, yanking her bikini bottom below her pubic bone.

Kali roared, an ancient scream strange to her lips but familiar. She swung the umbrella pole at him with all her power, over and over.

He gasped, laughed, still gripping her body like stolen fruit.

She thought of his ancestors harassing Willa and Charles; of plundered land, sanctioned rape, slave auctions, and lynchings.

It felt right to pull the dagger from its sheath, and plunge it deep into his abdomen.

His face registered shock as he crumpled. No howl. No regret.

She moved the blades up and down, side to side, puncturing and slicing through multiple organs.

She was efficient. Retribution. Reparation. Restitution. Truth and Reconciliation.

The blood gushed and pooled.

Kali heard her mother's voice reading from *Sula*—honeyed, righteous: "The presence of evil must be recognized, dealt with, outwitted, survived."

Heavy rain from the previous night had loosened the dunes. She worked fast, her hands steady, as if she'd done this before in another life. The beach swallowed him easily.

By the time the first jogger appeared on the horizon, only the ocean knew.

Adieu

The Words to Say It

Even as a trained interpreter, nothing prepared me for Arabic spoken by the old men of Iraq—juicy plums and ripe figs delivered by septuagenarians with hooded eyes and peppery mustaches.

I accidentally elbowed one of them, as he stood outside a cafe in Baghdad's Liberation Square.

"Sorry," I said in English, small, shriveled, almost useless. Then again in Arabic, "*Anā āsef*—I'm sorry."

"*Alzahrat aljamilat la yanbaghi 'an tasheur bial'asaf abdan*—A beautiful flower should never be sorry," he replied.

I waved whenever I spotted him on the square after that.

One day, I saw him standing alone. "*Ahlaan*—Hello," I said.

"*Ya Rouhi*—Oh my soul" he replied.

A helicopter, a loud whir, then an inferno.

He lay in three parts—head, torso and arms, legs. A precision strike.

His open eyes held me.

His blood was in my mouth.

It's been ten years since I've uttered a word in any language.

Hard Day's Night

"I'm goin' to get plastered. You comin'?"

Nina was as cut up about John Lennon's death as I was, as we all were. But if you'd put any of us up against a wall and given us a lit cigarette, we'd have confessed to being wretched long before that. For a whole bloody year anyway—since Margaret Thatcher swept into Number 10 with her stiff blonde helmet, her monumental handbags, and her strange ideas. The grocer's daughter wanted to spiff us up, turn England into a nation of peddlers. She vowed to crush the unions, and do away with welfare. The great British working class (that would be me, Nina, and our blokes, Mark and Alex) thought this a personal attack.

"Who does she think we are, American?" we grumbled. "She's learning all of it from that git Reagan innit?" Disturbed us no end, that the Iron Lady was taking advice and that from Mr. Star Wars.

"Too early for the pub, I'm set up here,' I let Nina in.

She followed me into the kitchen, hands crossed and hugging herself, cigarette clamped between her lips.

Nina and her bloke, Alex, lived next door in 17C, left of the piss-infected elevator. Mark and I lived in 17D, right of the piss-infected elevator.

"Light me one," I said, as I opened the fridge for beers. I was a stroppy cow without a fag in my hand, but I had no money on me since it was Thursday, and we didn't get our dole till Friday. It wasn't as if I'd wasted money on anything fancy either. Mark and I were careful: fifteen quid for the rent and 'electric, a score for the pub and smokes, pot if we got lucky, and the rest on food and toilet paper.

"Here," Nina broke the seal on a brand new pack of Embassy Reds.

She was good that way, none of that what's mine is mine Tory rubbish. But I did my share so things evened out.

Nina and Alex didn't cook. They lived on canned peaches, cereal, and biscuits. I always left our front door open so they could come in for shepherd's pie, stew, curry, or whatever was in the fridge and cupboards. I didn't mind cooking—kept me busy, stopped me from going mental. We all had our weekday obligations, and cooking was my lot. Mark went to the bookies to bet on everything—which ponce would win the Eurovision Song Contest, which horse at Hackney Downs, which bit of crumpet won Miss Universe, who'd win the World Cup playoffs. Alex went to the greyhound tracks in Leytonstone and stayed until the rabbit packed it in after the last race. Nina went to the launderette round the corner on Tottenham Road. Three times a week, Nina stuffed all our wash in two pillowcases, placed them in the basket of a shopping wheelie, and dragged the cart to Suds n' ope. The "H" in the purple neon sign had burnt out years ago. It didn't bother us though. We were Cockneys after all—we said "ello" and "fucking 'ell." What's H got to do with it?

"I thought John would always be around." Nina scraped the chair closer to the kitchen table, and planted her elbows on the red and white checkered cloth. "I took him for granted." Her straight, blonde hair, parted in the middle, fell over her face and down her shoulders like lace curtains.

"None of it makes any sense," I agreed, as I set two bottles of beer on the table.

"He was one of us, innit? Not one of them upper class gits like Elvis Costello and fucking Sting." Between sips, Nina held the bottle to her cheek.

"You've still got the songs." I consoled her.

"Not the same, is it?"

"It's life Nina. There'll be other songs."

"I counted on him. He could make a whole day go away."

We looked out the window in silence. It was an ugly sight. Five gray council high-rises that looked exactly like the one we lived in. In each of those buildings, there was a17C and a 17D arranged exactly the same way, occupied by people just like us lot—men who couldn't find work and lived on the dole, and women who found bits of work at the shops on the high street. If we needed a few extra quid, Nina and I would scope out the bakery, the butchers, the green grocers, the caf, and the fish n' chip shop. We skipped the Asians—the off-license, the curry shop, the newsstand. We weren't the kind to go Paki bashing or Dot busting, but working for Pakistanis and Indians would have done our heads in. We thought we were the bees fucking knees even though they were the ones who were loaded.. We'd chat up the non-Asian geezers just enough to get hired. But, as soon as they started acting up, copping a feel, trying to fiddle us, we'd pack it in.

"There's back to back Beatles on the radio," I said to Nina. "Shall I turn it on?"

"What for?" Nina replied. as she watched the ash of her cigarette grow into a talon.

Mark found us this way, sad for John Lennon, and for ourselves.

"Ready for a few?" he asked.

Serious bloke, my Mark. He'd been in art school when we met. His teachers at the Poly had said he was talented, but he dropped out and went on the dole. If he'd been lucky and found his way out of the East End, he would have been a real artist, a famous Cockney like Michael Caine. I used to encourage him all the time. Look at George Martin, I'd say. He was one of us, innit? He made it out. Took elocution lessons and that to sound all posh like. Do you fancy giving it a try?

"From here to there is harder than they say, innit?" Mark would say.

"Yeah." I would agree. After a while, I stopped talking about it 'cos we knew what we knew. Out of the East End and to the West End was only a tube ride, but it might as well have been on the bleedin' moon.

"I think there's one last beer left," I told Mark.

"I'll wait." He sat down next to Nina, as he pulled the week's pool forms from his back pocket. He studied the forms every

chance he got, weighing the odds for the week's matchups—
Arsenal vs. Nottingham Forest, Liverpool vs. Sheffield, Spurs vs.
Newcastle.

"I don't know why you bother. You're never going to win,
are you?" Nina said.

"I've got as much of a chance as the next bloke," Mark
retorted.

"What would you do with the money, luv?" I asked

"Just for starters, I'd set us up in a decent place. There's
one going for cheap down the road."

"Who would have thought it? Paradise at the end of our
street," Nina rolled her eyes at me.

We both cracked up. I was spineless that way. I never knew
why I joined Nina when she laughed at Mark, I didn't ever laugh at
Mark when we were alone. I mean we were great in the sack, which
was the important thing, innit? We tried new things all the time.
One morning we lay plastic bags on the bed, lathered ourselves in
Vaseline and shagged until lunchtime. Another time, we did it in a
bank vestibule near the night deposit vault, just on a lark.

"I'm dryer than the fucking Sahara. Let's go." Mark
stood up.

He was never more in his element than when he was at the
Red Lion—our local. He was happiest when he was all juiced up
on pints, high as a kite, playing darts or snooker, talking about
his picks for the pool.

"Where's Alex? Isn't he coming?" I asked Nina. I hoped he
wouldn't. Nina was a different self without Alex around.

"Can't you hear him? He's been playing Abbey Road since the morning news," Nina drew her thumbnail against the label of her bottle repeatedly. It was like a scab that wouldn't peel off, compressed into a tidy, serrated mass of pulp and gum. "He's stoked on something. Coke, stacks, somethin'."

"I'll get him," Mark said.

"Don't. He just whacked me across the face for trying," Nina said.

Mark and I knew better than to quiz Nina about it. It was a central part of their lives, Alex's rage. He hit Nina for interrupting him, saying the wrong thing, withholding money from him, nagging him, and loving him. We knew Alex had gone too far when Nina hid from us.

"This can't go on innit?" Mark and I would agree to speak to Alex. We would try to summon up the courage to tell Alex that it was crazy to hit the only good thing he had.

"Alright? Yeah, it has to be done, innit?"

But even before we had the chance to talk to Alex, we'd hear their bed creak and bump against their side of the dividing wall, loud moans, begging, negotiating for more, deeper, faster, harder.

The Red Lion was a botch up. The threadbare carpets buckled in places from rising damp. Gray masking tape patched the torn leather on barstools. The food was a bit dodgy, but you couldn't go wrong with a bottle. The whole neighborhood was already there sitting wake for John Lennon, when Nina, Mark, and I walked in. It was crowded—people leaning at the bar, seated at the booths ringing the room, standing about with their pints. The TV, which was usually set on Coronation Street or Crossroads, was off. The dartboard and snooker tables were standing all lonely like.

We waited for Sally, the barmaid, to pull us our pints. Sally was a slag. Her hair was bleached blonde like some 1950s RKO starlet. She wore gobs of makeup, and a pointy bra that made her knockers look enormous.

"Something more than John has been taken away from me. I don't know what it is," Sally said, as she placed our pints in front of us.

"He should have stayed in Liverpool, poor sod," Mark said.

An old geezer sitting at the bar, still wearing his raincoat but already paralytically drunk, ordered a bitter.

"What's this world coming to, eh?" Sally asked the old man.

"It'll just be a matter of time before everything goes under," the old man set his milky eyes on Sally.

Mark studied his forms, Nina sipped her drink and cooled her cheek, and I had a quiet think.

Later, when we went home, we found Alex in bed, flat on his back, eyes wide open, clutching his Abbey Road album. His lips were silvery and blue.

He left a note—Gave it a whirl. Load of cobblers. Ta very much.

Go Gentle Into This Good Morning

April 18, 2025

7:03 a.m.

Brooklyn, NY

My name is Elias Nathan Hollingwood. I am 102 years old. I was born in June of 1923 between the opening of Yankee Stadium and the death of President Warren Harding. This morning, I woke up at 5:02 a.m., the same time I have every day for the last eighty years. I put on my good sweater, the one with leather elbow patches, watered my plant, and made coffee. A physician from Coda Assisted Suicide is scheduled to arrive at 10 a.m. I have three hours left. Enough time to say what I've left unsaid.

I was born in Brooklyn in a fourth-floor walkup above a candy store. My parents were white, poor, religious, and ground down by misfortune and tragedy. They lost two sons during childbirth and two daughters before their second birthday. I lost them in inches—to alcoholism and depression. In 1936, my father died in his sleep on a May day. In June, my mother took a rope and her own life. I was claimed by child services and sent to the missionaries who transported me to Louisiana. My decade with the religious cured me of religion.

Pearl Harbor happened the day I turned eighteen. The next day, I enlisted in the Army, because the alternatives were penury and dead ends.

Let me say it plainly: I had inherited racism and bigotry from my parents, community, and society. I drank them with mother's milk and inherited them like a rusted pocketknife.

It was the war that cracked me open. During my rotation at a military hospital, I met the Navajo Coders and the Tuskegee Airmen—and marveled at their love for a country that had yet to love them back. I served with a man named Walter Boone, a Black mechanic from Mobile. He rebuilt engines like they were puzzles, fast and perfect. One night, under fire, he pulled me out of a crater and wrapped my shredded leg in a shirt that said "ALABAMA CHAMPIONS." He never said a word about it. When I came home, I wrote him a letter. I never sent it. I didn't know how. Maybe I was ashamed. Maybe I was afraid of the gratitude it required.

In 1950, I married Clara, a red-haired woman with a librarian's gaze and an Irish lilt. She made me feel lucky, that the God I didn't believe in had given me proof of divine intelligence. I was a good husband and attentive father to our two boys and twin girls.

Clara died in 1988 of a stroke. She was my girl, my bonnie lass. She had deserved opera and skylights. She died before I could give them to her.

In 1963, I watched President Kennedy's funeral, silent, on a black-and-white TV in a shop window. In 1968, I watched Dr. King's and then Robert Kennedy's funerals on a black-and-white

TV in our house, with the volume low. I remember thinking we failed them all, by demanding from them, not just their intelligence and vision, but their very lives.

While young Americans marched for Civil Rights and against the Vietnam War, I took refuge in neutrality. I didn't march. I didn't write letters. I just shook my head and told my children to stay in school. That's all. That's all I did. I lived in a world where men like me were the problem, and I let others do the solving.

I didn't think I would outlive my children. One son died in Vietnam, the other in the 9/11 flight that crashed into the Pentagon. One of my daughters was murdered by her husband, the other died of breast cancer. I am the last one standing—an old man in a quiet room, with history, memory, and nothing else.

The older you get, the more invisible you become. At 90, people call you "adorable." At 100, they say "God bless." At 102, they don't say anything—they assume you're already dead.

But I have been here and I have seen some things. I saw the moon landing. I saw three assassinations. I saw Nixon resign and Reagan charm a nation into forgetting. I saw towers fall and flags wave. I saw cities die coughing. I saw citizens storm their own Capitol in the name of a lie. I saw America twist itself into contradictions and turn lies into truths. And still I stayed quiet.

I joined the Hemlock Society in the 1990s. I liked the name. Hemlock, like Socrates. Death, but dignified. The organization changed names over the years, but the mission stayed: give people the right to leave.

When I turned 102 in Spring, I decided I was done. Not because of pain—I'm not in much. Not because I'm afraid—I lost my fear in '44.

Dylan Thomas left us a good poem with bad philosophy: *Do not go gentle into that good night, Old age should burn and rave at close of day; Rage, rage against the dying of the light.*

I beg to differ. I will go gentle into this good morning.

Because I'm done, because there's nothing more for me to do. My life has been lived. There are no more questions I want to ask or things I wish to see. I've outlived my usefulness. This is not surrender. This is symmetry.

To those who find this letter:

Live better than I did.

Don't raise your sons to fear softness.

Don't raise your daughters to serve silence.

Tell people when you're sorry.

Don't wait till they turn away to ask for forgiveness.

Say thank you with your whole heart.

Hold people.

Be tender with the people you love—they could vanish.

Let go of pride.

Do not confuse control with love.

Love without limit.

Be kind to the earth and the ocean.

And for God's sake, vote.

Vote like the world depends on it.

It is 9:52 a.m. now. The physician will be here soon. I am calm. I am warm. I have signed the forms and chosen music: Arvo Pärt's *Cantus in Memoriam Benjamin Britten*. My ashes go to the East River, if anyone remembers to carry them.

There's the knock at the door. My name is Elias Nathan Hollingwood. I was born in 1923. I die today at peace. Let this letter stand as my only monument.

Elias Nathan Hollingwood

End Notes

Some of these stories began as the first chapters of novels I haven't yet written. Others arrived whole, sudden, or small as seeds. A few were drawn from my earlier works—Liberty Landing (Mirare Press, 2018) and The Edge of the World (Mirare Press, 2007)—and reshaped for this condensed form.

I've lived in cities on three continents and love the sound of languages I do not speak. I've recast phrases I've heard or read and been moved by—especially from Arabic and Persian, both of which I find gorgeous, tender, and romantic. Some of those phrases appear in this collection, in their original languages and in translation—carrying their original ache and music.

In this new century of machines and social isolation, I've also been drawn to the question of what it means to feel—to long, to yearn, to be seen—across boundaries of flesh and code. Two stories in this book emerged from that inquiry. My research on artificial intelligence, emotional simulation, and human-machine connection was guided by ChatGPT, the large language model that helped me test and understand what it means for technology to mirror desire.

In some way, every character in these pages is a splinter of self or a trace of someone I once knew. Yet, *Small Worlds* is not a memoir but fiction—that is, life startled by imagination, shocked by fantasy and electricity.

Gail Vida Hamburg

Book Club Discussion Guide

Questions for Reflection and Discussion

- Many stories in Small Worlds explore self-invention. How do the characters use fantasy or deception to cope with their realities?

- Loneliness is a recurring theme. Which stories resonated with you in portraying isolation, and why?

- Several stories blur the lines between humor and tragedy. How does this tonal duality affect your reading experience?

- How do gender and power dynamics play out in relationships depicted in the collection?

- What role does longing—whether for love, recognition, or escape—play across the different sections?

- Rationale features characters justifying cruelty or moral lapses. Which story challenged your sense of empathy most?

- How does the collection's structure—short, compressed narratives grouped by theme—impact your engagement as a reader?

- The author references Mughal miniatures and sand paintings as inspirations. How does this visual metaphor enrich your reading of the stories?

- Do you see any connections between the brevity of these stories and the modern digital attention span?

- Which character or story stayed with you the longest, and why?

- If you could expand one story into a full-length novel, which would it be?

–   How does the collection as a whole redefine what makes a 'complete' story?

Behind *Small Worlds*: Author's Note for Readers

Small Worlds was born from my fascination with the art of compression. Just as Mughal miniature artists rendered epic tales on a few inches of canvas, and painters etched stories onto single grains of rice, I wanted to see how much emotional and narrative weight could be held in a small frame.

This collection invites you to linger over brief encounters, to witness how a moment, a glance, or a single choice can reveal an entire life. My hope is that these stories, while short, leave a lasting resonance.

For Writers: On Flash Fiction & Microfiction

Flash fiction and microfiction are literary forms that demand precision and depth in very limited space. Writing them is like carving intricate patterns into stone—every word must earn its place.

For writers, the challenge is to suggest a world beyond the text: to create characters with histories, desires, and futures in a few hundred words. It's an exercise in implication, restraint, and sharp emotional focus.

Try writing a flash story inspired by your own 'small world'—an everyday moment that holds deeper meaning.